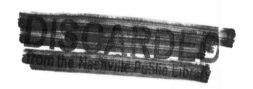

FEAR THE CONDOR

Also by David Nelson Blair
_____

The Land and People of Bolivia

C *FEAR THE* ONDOR

DAVID NELSON BLAIR

LODESTAR BOOKS

Dutton   New York

Library of Congress Cataloging-in-Publication Data

Blair, David Nelson.
Fear the condor / David Nelson Blair.—1st ed.
p. cm.
Summary: When her father and other Aymara Indians are sent to fight in the 1932 Bolivian war against Paraguay, Bartolina Ch'oke witnesses the beginning of changes in her people's way of life.
ISBN 0-525-67381-4
1. Aymara Indians—Juvenile fiction. [1. Aymara Indians—Fiction.
2. Indians of South America—Fiction. 3. Bolivia—History—
1879–1938—Fiction.] I. Title.
PZ7.B53738Fe   1992
[Fic]—dc20   91-46921
                                                                      CIP
                                                                       AC

Published in the United States by Lodestar Books, an affiliate of Dutton Children's Books, a division of Penguin Books USA Inc., 375 Hudson Street, New York, New York 10014

Published simultaneously in Canada by McClelland & Stewart, Toronto

Editor: Rosemary Brosnan
Designer: Richard Granald, LMD
Printed in the U.S.A.
First Edition
10 9 8 7 6 5 4 3 2 1

for Liliana Vargas

November 1932, Maya

I never once heard Doña Hilde moan about the lazy brothers Hail and Wind and Frost. Instead, she worried about dust. When she came to live inside the strong walls of the hacienda house, she brought her war against dust to Masuru. She wanted a girl to chase even the least bit that sneaked into her realm. So she sent Fortunato Herrán to get me.

Before the sun came up that morning, Father woke me. "Bartolina, help me with the crops."

I curled on my reed mat. I pulled my blanket tight around me, just for the smallest instant. Grandmother, lying close beside me, caught me with her scolding. "Don't be lazy!"

I rose quickly. Thief shoots wanted to choke our young beans and shrink our potatoes. "If we let them," Father always said, "they'll take our whole plot without giving back a single thing to eat." So we had to bend over and pull up each one.

I dressed in a top and long skirts of tightly woven alpaca wool, then followed Father past the blanket that hung over our doorway. My open hide sandals let the lazy brother Frost find my feet. Even in the green season, he came teasing until the sun chased him. Father pulled down the pointed earflaps of his cap and held his poncho tight around him.

I gasped when a cry startled the most fearing of my souls. Father laughed because anyone could tell it was a lamb's bleat. An animal pen stood close beside each of the family houses in that part of Masuru.

Above the hacienda, the sky began its awakening, but slowly. When we reached our plot, seeing was still difficult, but we couldn't leave our work until later. Then, Grandmother would need my help with the marketing. Father would have to take his turn working the *patrón*'s wide fields.

I finished two rows of broad beans and counted those still left. *"Maya, paya, quimsa, pusi, pheska, sojta, pakallko."*

"Just keep pulling," Father scolded.

Fortunato found us bent over our crops. "Donato Ch'oke," he called to Father, "where are the woven blankets your wife owes to the *patrón*?"

I trembled, but on that open ground I couldn't hide. So I just put my head low. I knew Fortunato was speaking a trick.

He had wide shoulders and strong arms. Even when he was young, anyone could see his size. Don Luciano, Masuru's administrator, noticed him the same day Fortunato's people came hungry to the hacienda. He gave Fortunato's father a sheep so that the new family wouldn't starve before the first harvest. Then, as soon as Fortunato was old enough to crack a whip, Don Luciano told him he'd work as a *mayordomo*. "You'll help me keep order for the *patrón*."

Father faced Fortunato. "My wife died five years ago. You know that!" His angry voice frightened me. I watched the whip coiled and hanging at Fortunato's belt. I'd seen it bite men—and once a woman.

"A terrible shame, Donato. But you have to start thinking

about your obligations. The *patrón* still lets you use a house and this whole plot. What does he get back?"

"I work hard in his fields. My wife's mother gives him woven goods."

"Do you know Anastasio Barrios?"

"We all know him, Fortunato. What do you want?"

"Anastasio works hard, too. And he's got two sons here serving as field hands. Another works on the *patrón*'s plantation. Let me think. How many daughters does he have weaving?"

"Fortunato, if I stand talking and don't tend my crops, my family won't eat. If I don't rethatch my roof, the next rain will soak my sleeping mat. Tell me what you want."

I stood wishing that Father would calm himself. Why risk provoking the *mayordomo?*

"It's lucky for you that Don Luciano's new wife needs a girl to keep things clean. At last Bartolina will be doing something useful. Three days each week, you'll send her to the hacienda house to serve Doña Hilde."

"Three days' service from a girl of ten?"

Father's shout sent my eyes back to that whip. I breathed again only when Fortunato let it rest. He spoke no more fiercely than a market woman asking three white potatoes for an arm's length of cloth. "That's still only two people working and a cross old woman weaving, but Don Luciano is a good man. If Bartolina works hard, he'll probably let you stay."

Fortunato turned to me. "Be sure you're at the hacienda house tomorrow, just at sunrise." He walked off without another word.

Father pulled up more thief shoots, but he mumbled angrily and didn't work so fast as before. My fearing soul still worried. Maybe Father would tell me to mind my sheep and forget the hacienda house. Maybe Fortunato would come raging at me in the pastures. *What then?*

Father stood straight and looked to the east. A row of great mountains stood black against the sky. The biggest, Illampu, tried to hold back the sun.

Beyond, two days' walking along steep, winding trails, lay the Yungas. Father went there as a boy and served for a year as mule tender on the *patrón*'s plantation. "Pumas still roam there," he told me once. "The land is the richest, but it's all on slopes. A man can't stand straight." He told of trees and trees that hid the sky. He moaned about tiny flying beasts, uncountable thousands of them, every single one forever trying to bite.

That mountain row ran as far as I could see—the whole length of Kollasuyo. But Father had no traveling tales that followed the peaks north or south. His only journey had been the one to the Yungas.

I pulled more thief shoots, but I kept worrying about Fortunato's order and Father's anger. Once I pulled up a bean plant with a clump of thieves. Father shouted, "Girl, each mistake robs us of food!"

I almost cried, but Father settled himself. "Watch me, Bartolina." He worked his finger into the dry soil. Then he stood the bean shoot in the hole. He knew just how deep to set it in. He knew just how tightly to pack the earth around it. "Maybe Pachamama will still let it grow."

"Please, Pachamama," I prayed.

Father straightened, this time looking south. Farthest in the distance stood the peak Illimani. He watched it for a moment, then shook his head. "We can't risk trouble. If we lost this plot, we'd have no way to feed ourselves. What then? You'll have to do what Fortunato says."

Only then did my fearing soul rest.

November 1932, *Paya*

O n the smooth stones between our house and the cookhouse, I braided Grandmother's black hair into two long tails. She did mine the same way, but all through it she spoke only two words, "Hold still." An anger had seized her the moment Father told her about my new service. I was relieved that she hadn't been close when Fortunato came.

We spread our shawls to prepare for market. Grandmother only spoke to scold or warn. "Be careful with those *chicha* jars." During the ice season, Father had carefully shaped those jars from clay, then fired them on a hillside. They'd bring something at market. I carefully wrapped them in the woven bags and caps left over after giving the *patrón* his share.

I held up one special cap. A little puma face decorated each earflap. Grandmother had shown me how to weave dark and light wool together to make the images, and I'd done it just right. Father had smiled and admired it. I felt proud when he said, "You have a strong weaving soul."

"Can't we save just this one for Father?"

Grandmother's answer was fierce. "Donato has a cap!" Then she explained with calmer words. "That's your best one. Keeping it means throwing away what it can bring at market."

We folded the corners of our shawls so that nothing would drop. I pointed to a wide clay bowl. "Maybe I can carry that, too."

Grandmother shook her head. "Burdens grow heavier with each step, Bartolina. Be wise like the llama, who refuses too great a load. We'll take that bowl next time."

We began toward Cauquimarca. We passed the hacienda house, standing penned in by its wall. I could see only the rows of little curved plates that made its roof. They were dull red—like oca, the little sweet potato.

The road turned away from the house, but I kept looking back, wondering about my new service. I'd taken my first close look at Doña Hilde only the morning before—on All Souls' Day. In a narrow black dress, she stood in a part of the cemetery just across the road from the Ch'oke graves. Her hat had the widest brim I'd ever seen. Over it, then knotted under her chin, a thin cloth held it safe against the lazy brother Wind. She'd come with Don Luciano, who knelt at the grave of his first wife. His three sons knelt beside him, praying for their mother. Doña Hilde prayed, too, but she didn't kneel. Maybe her fine dress cloth would have been spoiled.

When I kept looking back toward the hacienda house, Grandmother pointed the other way. "Cauquimarca is there."

Halfway, she wanted to rest. We sat against the mud and stone wall that surrounds the *patrón*'s pasture. Just then someone shouted. "You there!" A *mayordomo* looked over the wall from ten steps away. "We have enough repairs without lazy sloths trying to push the wall down."

I began to move that instant. I wanted to stand away and calm his anger. Before I could, Grandmother seized my arm.

She pulled me back to where I'd been sitting. I could only think of that *mayordomo*'s whip.

Of all Grandmother's souls, her confronting soul was the strongest. Whenever it seemed that the lazy brother Hail might beat down young bean shoots, she'd rush out under the wide sky and burn hot peppers to drive him away.

Her black eyes went small as they found the *mayordomo*. "We rest," she told him. "A woman and a girl sitting do not break down walls."

Maybe she'd been looking the other way when that *mayordomo* first spoke. Maybe he hadn't known he was shouting at Julia Caranavi. When he did see, he just stood looking stupid. Grandmother yawned a bit and closed her eyes.

Finally the *mayordomo* spoke again. "I've got better things to do right now than bother you, Julia. But I'm coming back soon. You'd better hope I don't catch you here."

Grandmother didn't move or speak. She didn't open her eyes. I don't know if the *mayordomo* came back, but if he did, it was after we'd finished our rest.

At the far western edge of Masuru, we left the road at the cemetery, which took in all the dead from the town and nearby haciendas. We walked just outside the low cemetery wall. Grandmother pointed over it toward the Ch'oke graves we'd visited the day before. "You should be proud, Bartolina. Ch'oke is the oldest family at Masuru."

We knelt at a grave outside the wall. It lay among those of thieves, though Juan Caranavi had *not* been a thief. "Bartolina, you can always kneel at this grave without worry. What does it matter if a *mayordomo* notices? He'll just say: 'She's Juan's granddaughter. It's to be expected.' He won't even bother telling the administrator."

She'd said the same thing at the grave the day before. We'd been the only ones to visit—in daylight. But Masuru people had come sneaking in the darkness. They'd left woven flowers and bits of coca all around Grandfather Juan's grave. Seeing these tributes, Grandmother smiled just for a moment, the only time she smiled that day. Then she spoke angrily, telling Grandfather about my service. I let my head fall. I was glad when we went back to the road.

Just beyond the cemetery, a stone church stood alone on the east side of Cauquimarca's market square. Its front wall reached above its roof and formed two archways that stood higher than anything else around. Each held a bell, open to the sky.

Buildings filled the square's other sides—five or six on each one. One place had beds for travelers. The next served them food, and they could leave their animals in the stable across the square. Another place served *chicha*, the corn beer. Men from Masuru and Cauquimarca and all around went there to drink and repeat the news that market women brought.

A store at one corner sold strong sacks and fine scarves of bright colors. It had a stand that swayed back and forth, and people put coca or bits of silver on its little trays to find out how much they had. Like a llama, it always knew its load, and people trusted it more than they trusted one another.

Every market day, tens and tens of market women came to Cauquimarca and filled the square with bright blankets. On some they laid grapes, palm leaves, and big sacks of coca leaves from the Yungas. On others were tin cups and plates from all across Kollasuyo.

"Have you heard the news?" a market woman showing peppers asked Grandmother. "They've pushed us right out of Boquerón."

I'd never heard of Boquerón, so why say "us"? Grandmother didn't worry herself with it. Instead, she took up a pepper to test its scent.

~ 8 ~

My eyes went searching westward along the road to Achacachi. Not once in my life had I walked past the square, not even to the houses of Cauquimarca people just beyond. But I was curious about something standing there. It seemed to be the tiniest possible house, all black. Together with its small pen, it somehow crouched on legs as round as the moon.

I'd seen trucks before, but always rushing in the distance. They made a terrible bellowing. Little viscachas nearby would shake their furry tails and rush to their burrows. Even the dust on the road fled when a truck passed. My cousin Dionisio said that one had killed a sheep near Huarina—just in an instant, before anyone could stop it.

This one stood silent. Sleeping? Or watching back at me with two big eyes?

The truck was outside the last house before the open road. People had begun calling that place the Baptist mission, and twice I'd seen the man who lived there. From a distance, I could see only that he stood very tall.

Market women said that the Baptist spoke against our priest, Padre Roberto. They said he'd been driven away from Pucarani by townspeople who didn't want his mission there.

I knew not to ask questions. With stern eyes, Father had warned me the month before: "Don't let anyone see you paying any special mind to that Baptist."

Father's brother, Uncle Jacinto, told me almost the same thing. "It wouldn't be good if people started saying that Ch'okes went in and out of the Baptist mission."

Maybe someone would see me looking! I quickly turned back into the square and went sniffing at fish. The fish woman spoke about the same place that worried the pepper woman—Boquerón. "All those men couldn't hold it," she told a Cauquimarca woman. "They say the Guaraní fight like devils. What will Salamanca do now?"

I didn't care about Boquerón. Instead, I wanted to know something I couldn't ask about. If seeing the Baptist might mean trouble, why did Uncle risk sending my cousin Dionisio to the mission?

November–December 1932

The next day, an iron gate intervened against me. It wouldn't let me reach the hacienda house. I saw no rope like the one I untied to open Father's animal pen. My hands pushed and pulled, pushed and pulled. I remembered Fortunato's order—and his whip. Tears fell down my face.

I thought of Mother. I remembered her hands on my shoulders once when I was very small. We'd been standing at the grave of Casimiro, my brother, who lived his whole life in just one green season.

"Remember the time that Padre Roberto poured water on Casimiro?" Mother had asked. We'd been lucky. The priest came to Masuru only two months after Casimiro's birth. Mother knelt and turned me to face her. "A baptized child goes straight to heaven. D'you see? Casimiro is completely innocent, so there's no doubt. He's already an *angelito* sitting among the saints. You can pray to him."

"Not to the Virgin of Copacabana?"

"To her, too. But she's for all of Kollasuyo. She has a thousand shrines and hears prayers and prayers. But to Casimiro, your prayers are special. You're his only sister in the world, and he'll listen especially to you."

So, trembling at that iron gate, I appealed to the one tiny

saint who would hear me day or night. Just then, I heard heavy footsteps inside the wall.

"Help me!" I called. "This gate won't let me pass."

Something like a fork jumped, and the gate swung open. "Don't you know how to lift a latch, girl?"

The man asking had a face that seemed too long. There didn't seem to be enough brownness to it. But these *wirajjocha* looks weren't what stopped my breath in an instant. Instead, I worried about who his eyes had found. Never before had Don Luciano spoken straight to me.

The administrator was the first person I'd ever seen riding a horse or wearing a pistol. He could decide in a moment what family was allowed to settle at Masuru. He could just as easily expel one. And when his first wife died, we learned that he could summon a priest at will!

I couldn't speak. I just stood looking at the thick black hair that made a little roof over his lips.

"Manuela!" he called back to the house. He didn't wait for an answer. A moment later he went striding toward the stable.

"Bartolina?" I recognized Manuela Zavaleta coming around the house. She cooked for the administrator. "Come on, girl." She seemed cross, then and most times.

Inside the wall, my sandals no longer touched the soil. I walked on squares—like our patio stones, but as smooth as pond water when the air is still. They fit perfectly together. Pachamama couldn't send even the thinnest blade of grass between them. The hacienda house had a heavy wooden door carved with hummingbirds among *kantuta* petals and small, narrow leaves. Black iron guarded glass windows, but those bars weren't straight. They pretended to be flowers and leaves.

We didn't go through the carved door. I followed Manuela toward the back. "What Spanish words do you know, Bartolina?" she asked.

"Spanish words?"

She stopped that instant and faced me. "I hope you know enough to call the administrator's wife Doña Hilde or Señora."

I knew *doña,* and I decided right then to remember the other word. "Yes, Manuela."

"Just remember, you can speak Aymara words to the administrator, but they're no good with this new señora."

Why would words be no good with someone? Before I could ask, Manuela turned away. I followed her into the part of the house where she cooked. This one room was bigger than our house and cookhouse together. Iron pans hung from one wall—some deep, some shallow and wide. Below, a large knife lay on a table where Manuela had been chopping meat, potato, and spices. The richest feast day had never smelled so good.

Across the room, a huge black box stood on short legs. I could feel its warmth and wondered how such a thing could be. The burning smell told me. Twisty *yareta* roots fed a cook fire *inside.*

Manuela pulled two sticks down from the wall, one short, one long. They ended in huge flowers, but with feathers instead of petals. "Come," said Manuela.

We went to a great room. Its gray floor seemed to be a single stone, smooth except for the smallest ripples. A heavy table stood among eight chairs. All were dark, yet they still shone. I touched one and felt wood, somehow made so smooth that no splinter would ever bite.

Far down the room sat a chair longer than a sleeping mat. There were other chairs and low tables—more wood. I'd never seen so much wood. And the window had clothes.

Long robes reached down its sides. Behind them, spread wide over the whole window, hung a white blanket so thin that I could see through it. It seemed to be woven from smoke.

"This room has to be kept clean." Manuela put the long featherstick in my hand. "Start high, where the ceiling meets the walls. If you leave any dust, you'll have to go back again." I also had to run the long featherstick over the room's corners. Then I had to chase the dust from everything in the room with the short featherstick.

I worked, but I also wanted to see everything. That room had storing places with doors of glass. Candles stood three together on stands of silver. A man with *wirajjocha* looks gazed down from a part of the wall that seemed to be a pasture with sheep. I knew it was all an image, like my puma faces, yet it was completely perfect. Looking for the least trace of a stitch, I wondered how it had been woven. And who had ever seen a *wirajjocha* man tending his own sheep?

Hearing footsteps, I turned. "Ah, Bartolina." Doña Hilde, as tall as Father, stood facing me, with Manuela just behind her. The señora's eyes were missing their blackness—they peered brown into mine. I looked down, to the very straight end of her skirt, and my eyes found the closest, smallest stitches I'd ever seen. The cloth surprised me even more. It somehow held the images of a thousand tiny flowers. They didn't seem to be woven in at all. They were just there.

Doña Hilde kept speaking. That gave me a fright because her words wouldn't let themselves be understood. I thought of Padre Roberto's prayers—priest words that are only for the Virgin and the saints. I began thinking. Hadn't Manuela spoken of "Spanish words" and "Aymara words"?

Finally the cook waved her hand at the shepherd's image. She spoke with the familiar words I'd heard all my life.

Aymara words? We're Aymara people, I thought, so I decided they must be. "The señora says she admires you for looking to the Savior. She chooses you for service because she saw you praying so devoutly on All Souls' Day."

It was true. An old widow, Concevida Cáceres, had told me that the prayers of children are heard first. She gave me sweet cakes to pray for her dead. I asked Pachamama to give them plentiful crops. I asked Saint Michael to let them sit among the saints. I asked the grandfather of the great peak Illampu to spoil the luck of their enemies. I especially asked Casimiro to visit Concevida's mother, for she had died a lonely widow.

"The señora says she wants only a faithful girl working in this proper Christian home.... Give back a smile, Bartolina." With Doña Hilde near, Manuela hid her crossness. "Thank her for her admiration. Say 'Gracias, Doña Hilde.'"

I repeated the strange word as best I could.

The señora nodded. Then Manuela became stern. "Now, don't forget your work."

After I had chased dust from the chairs in the sitting place, Doña Hilde came looking. Right away she called Manuela away from her busy chopping.

Those chairs had many carvings, like that heavy door. "You have to blow, Bartolina," the cook scolded. I blew hard, and more dust flew from the deep carved spaces. "Don't be lazy about your work, or it will have to be done over."

Doña Hilde came again and again. Most times she found fault and called Manuela. Each time, the cook was more cross. "Girl, you'd better learn the Spanish words—and quickly!"

I was not the only Ch'oke to come through the iron gate to the hacienda house. Each morning my Grandfather Alfonso brought stream water for the administrator and his family. He'd carry and carry, enough times to allow for a day's washing and cooking. Then he'd put down his buckets and rest in the sun just outside Manuela's cooking place.

Grandfather was the oldest person I knew. Father and Uncle were his sons, and he lived with Uncle's family in a house near Father's. I loved him because he had just one desire—to please. Of all his souls, his obliging soul was the strongest. It could pull all the deep lines of his face into a wide smile. Grandfather wanted happiness for every single person who came into his sight. For Don Luciano and Doña Hilde he even had a special obliging voice, high and pleasant like a young boy's.

While he rested, Grandfather told me things about the house. Men far to the south dug silver from mountains, made it pure, and beat it into those candlestands. All that wood had come over winding, steep trails from the Yungas. "The chairs and tables belong to the *patrón*," he said. "They're from the days before the *patrón* had the Yungas plantation or his La Paz house. A little part of Masuru was his only land, and he lived in this house himself."

I sat wondering about the *patrón*. Sometimes he visited, but even less often than Padre Roberto. I'd seen him close up only once. I must have been very small because I remember no face, only Mother saying, "Look, the *patrón*." Don Luciano had been there, too. He took a clump of soil, breaking it in his hand and letting it fall as dust. The *patrón* watched, but he kept his arms folded across his chest. He never once let his hands touch the soil.

The señora allowed me this lazy sitting with Grandfather because he taught me Spanish words. He surprised me by saying that I already knew some—*hacienda* and *patrón* and *padre*. Yet how could I remember a Spanish word for every

Aymara word? It seemed impossible, especially since Doña Hilde was quick to call me back into the house.

At first I only chased dust, but I seemed to chase it forever. Beyond the big eating and sitting room were rooms for washing. There was a room where Don Luciano and Doña Hilde slept. Don Luciano's sons had a room for sleeping. And there was a special place, the *oficina*, where the administrator sat when he wasn't out riding.

Before I finished the last room, more dust would sneak into the first. Maybe Rómulo, the youngest son, would come stamping through. Dust and dust leaped off his boots every time. I learned to work quickly because I wanted to help Father with the thief shoots. I wanted to watch animals with my cousins as many days as I could, but Doña Hilde found new things to hold me to my three days. I learned to polish wood and silver. I learned to clean glass.

I'd been working in the house for a month when Manuela started me serving coca tea. Twice each day Doña Hilde wanted some from a little drinking jar that sat on a plate. The first time I brought it, Rómulo came in, chased the dust off his clothes, and drank some with her.

I'd only just begun learning Spanish words, so I didn't know what they were saying. Yet I heard "Boquerón." I remembered that name, but from where? Then, when I was taking the tea jars and plates away, I heard "Salamanca."

Ya-ya-YA-ya. Ya-ya-YA-ya. D'you hear? *Sa-la-MAN-ca* is like a wordless song that we girls chant on feast days when the men play tall drums and reed pipes. That's what let me remember the talk of the market women.

January 1933, Maya

I stood on a hill—huge to climb, but still only a toe of the giant peak Illampu. Far to the west I saw the hacienda house and its stable. Near them, the Masuru families' hundred houses stood in five clumps. Beyond, the *patrón's* walled lands reached all the way to Cauquimarca.

I thought I could see all the world. My eyes followed two streams, the only ones that let us chase our thirst. They twisted close to every one of Masuru's seven thin trees. One passed the fishing town Huarina. The other passed the big market town Achacachi. Only far in the distance did they find what they searched for, the wide waters of Lake Titicaca.

I stood wondering if the streams asked the trees to point the way toward the lake. Just then Basilia, my oldest cousin, yelled hard. "Condor!"

That condor sneaked out of Illampu's morning shadows. He seemed to be all wings and black feathers, already passing close above when I first saw him. Then I saw a collar of white. I saw the paleness in his head and long, naked neck.

Before my heart beat again, I was running down the hill. Usually a condor wants dead or dying beasts in the mountains, maybe an old vicuña. If he finds none, he sometimes takes a small Masuru lamb.

"What would we do without wool and meat?" Father asked whenever he sent me to watch his sheep.

"You must not let them stray," Grandmother had said only that morning, "not even one!" Her hard eyes scolded, even before I started toward the pasture with Father's six sheep.

I quickly circled the flock. I drove the sheep into a close pack, but I gasped when I counted only five. I whirled, looking and looking for Father's smallest lamb, the one that liked to wander.

It stood a hundred steps away. That condor had already begun his swoop toward it. I went completely still, like a toad pretending to be a stone while a teasing boy runs past.

"Yaaaaaa!" This was Basilia shouting. She held her skirts and raced toward the lamb. The condor passed only the height of a man over my cousin and the lamb. I saw his red comb, proudly cocked forward like a crown. His beak and talons could have torn through any hide. I was ashamed for leaving my cousin to stand against the condor, but I'd been afraid to offend him.

A moment later Basilia took up the lamb and rushed back to protect her own sheep. At first I thought she wanted to keep it as a tribute for her intervention. I thought I'd have to tell Father—with Grandmother listening to every single word. "Basilia!"

She turned, just for a moment. "See to the rest of your sheep, Bartolina!"

The others wouldn't stay close together, not even with that condor still near. I circled the sheep again, shooing them into a safe pack.

My two cousins began coming toward me, but only slowly.

They couldn't leave their animals unprotected and had to drive the flocks ahead of them. Adela reached me first.

She was my same age, and we were best friends. When we were small, we pretended that we were mothers to the sheep. We still always sat together for singing on feast days.

Her father's big alpaca walked with her. Uncle Jacinto was proud of its size. Except for its thick, curly wool, someone might have thought it was a stout llama. The condor wouldn't come near with such a beast standing close. Maybe that's why Adela put its rope into my hand.

Basilia arrived scolding. "Bartolina, you have to keep watching! Haven't I warned you about the condor whenever we're this close to the mountains? And what about foxes? If your sheep fall prey, what are you going to eat before the harvest comes in? What are you going to wear when those lazy brothers Frost and Wind conspire?"

"We need *yareta* for our cook fire. I climbed the hill to spy for some."

"You sat lazy, looking and looking at the lake. I saw you. Did you think the fish would come sneaking after your sheep?" She shooed Father's lamb back to me.

I felt ashamed. Things were already more difficult for my cousins. They had to watch my father's sheep on days that I went to the hacienda house. I began to weep. Just then, I think to mock me, the condor above made the sun wink.

I wanted to herd in the near pasture, closer to home, but its grass had been grazed right down to the soil. Every Masuru family had a flock eating hungrily. We had to come into the hills of the far pasture—and risk tempting the condor and fox.

Basilia saw my fear. She spoke more softly. "We won't separate again today. We'll keep all the animals close." She looked around at the clumps of grass, well apart in the dry soil. "But we'll have to keep them moving. Grass in one spot won't last long with all of them together."

I was relieved, at least for that moment. Basilia was wise about herding. For months she had been carefully explaining things to Adela and me—when to move the flock, how to help a ewe give birth. "As soon as you can, pierce the lamb's ear and tie in the earmark with the special Ch'oke knot. Red and green threads mark Father's animals; red and blue ones mark Uncle Donato's."

Still, her explaining made me worry. It let me remember that Basilia wouldn't be in the pastures much longer. A *mayordomo* had said that she must help with the *patrón's* next harvest. Uncle answered this with loud shouting, but what could he do against the administrator?

We moved our herds among the hills many times. Once I gasped. I recognized an especially rocky crest not far away. Until then, I hadn't seen how close we were to the evil hill Iquiña. It stood high enough that Grandmother had once pointed to it from our house. "You must never go there, Bartolina," she told me. She explained that the souls of unbaptized babies wandered along Iquiña's slopes. Below the crest, those same slopes lay thick with the moss that grows above *yareta* roots, but no one ever went there to dig.

I looked beyond to Illampu. Already that morning I'd offered a pinch of shredded coca leaf to the peak's grandfather. I always did when I took sheep deep into his realm. But standing so close to Iquiña, standing below that soaring condor, I needed to be certain. I dropped another pinch to keep the mountain grandfather's favor.

I thought about my other cousin, Dionisio. He still watched the animals, but only on the days when I worked at the hacienda house. On the other days, he did his sneaking to visit the Baptist.

Before, we had all herded together. Sometimes Dionisio pretended to be the lazy brother Hail and chased us among the sheep, all of us laughing the whole time. Then he and Basilia would let us little girls nap, knowing they could manage against danger themselves. When we woke up, we sometimes pointed at Illampu's cap, which Adela said was made of snow. Other times we sneaked up on furry viscachas sunning themselves on rocks. How close could we get before they whistled and shook their tails angrily?

I longed for those days of laughing and running, of wondering how snow could be woven into a cap.

That condor still wanted Father's lamb. He stayed above us, even past the time of the highest sun. We moved westward to the lowest hills, and finally he disappeared. I never saw him leaving, and I was just as afraid *not* seeing him.

Soon after, I heard a deep, faraway thunder. From a hilltop, I could see dust leaping high from the road to Cauquimarca. Never had I seen a truck come to Masuru, yet there came two together. Adela pointed to a man riding hard from the *patrón's* fields. "It must be Don Luciano," she said. "He's galloping to confront them."

That scared me. The trucks seemed big and powerful. They might be vicious, like the one that killed the sheep near Huarina. Yet they faced our strong administrator, who could order fierce punishment for trespassers. Maybe a battle would start right then.

Father's wandering lamb bleated. I thought those trucks had tricked me into looking away for too long, but the herd was safe. Just the same, I carefully checked the sky for the condor and the hills for a sneaking fox.

When I looked westward again, I could see a mule tender leading Don Luciano's horse to the stable. Those two green trucks rested near the hacienda house, and everything seemed calm. The administrator stood talking with men from the trucks—and Doña Hilde also. "Don Luciano wouldn't let her stand there if those trucks were dangerous," Basilia said.

Soon the trucks bellowed away without the slightest harm to anyone. I kept watch over my flock and searched the sky and the pasture, all the time wondering where the next danger would appear. I never once thought to worry about that little song: *Sa-la-MAN-ca.*

January 1933, Paya

W alking home, I wanted only to put Father's sheep into their pen, away from danger. Then I could settle myself and eat bird stew and mash from the bitter potato. I didn't worry again about the trucks—until I found the Ch'okes all gathered outside Father's house.

Grandmother held her hardest eyes on Grandfather. He faced her, explaining and explaining. Father sat still against the house. Uncle sat beside him, arms crossed over his big chest.

Grandmother turned away from Grandfather, just as if he'd said nothing. "There's a cave under Iquiña," she told Father just as I got close enough to hear. "I can show you."

Father didn't look at her. He just sat, his fist tightly closed. I shut the animals into the pen and sat beside him.

"Julia, what's the use?" asked Grandfather.

"I'll say Donato went to Sorata. I'll say he has a sick cousin there."

"He'll have to come back sometime. What then?"

They all went silent. I finally dared to speak. "What's wrong?" Their looks frightened me.

Father answered: "Thieves have taken land in the Chaco. Men are needed to drive them away. Soldiers in trucks told Don Luciano that twenty Masuru men must help."

"Your father is one called to go," said Grandfather. "The trucks are returning for him in three days."

"Where's this Chaco?" I asked. "Is it the *patrón*'s land?"

Father thought a moment. "Maybe yes."

"I've never heard of him having land in any Chaco," said Grandmother.

"Julia's right," said Uncle. "I heard Don Luciano say that the land must be taken back for Bolivia."

"Who's Bolivia?" I asked.

"Why should Donato owe more service?" Grandmother asked.

No one answered, but while Father tried to decide what to do, my two grandparents spoke angrily against each other.

"Julia, the administrator says Donato must go."

"He can hide."

"The soldiers said that any man who doesn't appear will be tracked down."

"Alfonso, soldiers know nothing of Iquiña's cave. Not even the *patrón* knows of it. We learned that ... before." Her last word was only a whisper.

"Why speak of unhappy times?"

"Unhappy? Alfonso, those were most honorable days!"

Grandfather made his voice calm. "We'd best think about what our days will be like if Donato *is* found."

"The soldiers won't look for long. Thieves in this Chaco need chasing; they won't waste time searching our hills."

"But Julia, there will be trouble with the administrator whenever Donato returns." He looked at Uncle and spoke so that I could barely hear his words. "We're risking enough by sending Dionisio to that Baptist. Why take another chance? We could be expelled. What then?"

Grandmother answered. "Don Luciano knows that Donato works hard. He knows that you carry water and that

Bartolina cleans his house. Any trouble for Donato will pass quickly."

"Maybe that's true, Donato," Uncle said.

"But why take the risk?" asked Grandfather. "Go with the trucks, Donato. Then we'll have the administrator's favor even more. Then maybe we'll get by, maybe even if there's trouble over Dionisio."

Grandmother's voice became fiercer. "Donato is my son-in-law, and Don Luciano knows he *must* respect me."

"Because of Juan?" Grandfather held back his obliging soul like never before. "Julia, let your man rest!"

"Juan will never rest while . . ." Grandmother never finished. She just stopped speaking and turned away. I followed to the cookhouse to help with the stew. Darkness fell with nothing more said about the trucks.

The next day, Father said he wouldn't defy the administrator. "We'll be many," he told Grandmother. "We'll chase these thieves and forget them before things get busy with the harvest."

On the morning the trucks came again, Father stood waiting among the chosen men at the administrator's gate. Most Masuru people went looking—other men, women, and even the smallest children. I had my service, but seeing Manuela go, I followed. Only Grandmother and a few others stayed away. They wouldn't have anything to do with the soldiers.

Two trucks came together—both green, like the ones I'd seen before. One had a pen already filled with men, maybe from Macata, just to the north. Grandfather left his buckets and stood talking among the twenty men who were leaving. Small children came looking and sniffing at the trucks, which smelled like strong *chicha*. The bravest crept up and touched them before running back a few steps.

I saw Father and ran to stand with him while a soldier with a rifle called names. Doña Hilde saw me but never thought to scold me about my work. It almost seemed like a feast day.

Father's name was called. I hugged him. Uncle and Grandfather hugged him, and he climbed into the truck. Just then I felt bad. I didn't like seeing him in a pen.

Then Uncle and other men took up reed pipes and played feast songs. The trucks howled and began to move. Someone called out: "Remember Boquerón! Give those Guaraní a good kick!"

"Why speak of the Guaraní devils at Boquerón just now?" I asked Uncle.

"Boquerón is in the Chaco," he said. "Those thieves you've heard about *are* the Guaraní. But you mustn't be afraid. You saw how many men went off to chase them."

That made me braver, but when Uncle peered after the trucks a moment later, his eyes seemed to speak against his words.

I didn't go straight home after my service. The long days of the green season gave me time to climb Chuyma, a low hill and the only one in the near pasture. From its crest, my eyes followed the road the trucks had taken to the south. Far beyond Masuru it lost itself among hills.

The level plain of Kollasuyo stretched and stretched alongside the line of mountain peaks. There seemed no end to it. Was the Chaco out there somewhere? Or was it on the other side of the mountains? I didn't know.

Still, those trucks had moved so quickly, maybe quickly enough to go anywhere and back in a long day. I looked for fleeing dust along the road, for any sign that the trucks were returning. I saw none. When the sun was ready to hide itself somewhere far past Lake Titicaca, I hurried home.

"Why do you come so late?" Grandmother asked.

I told her.

"Child! Who said your father would go and come back in a day?" Then her voice went softer. "Bartolina, this thing will take time." Her worry was stronger than her anger.

February–March 1933

A month later, I told a woman selling fish that Father would be home soon. "We'll be able to forget those Chaco thieves before things get busy with the harvest." That market woman laughed in my face.

The next day, Doña Hilde found me sitting on the floor by the eating table. She saw my tears and called Manuela.

"Are you hurt?" the cook asked.

I shook my head.

"Are you sick?"

I shook my head.

"Has someone died?"

"No, Manuela."

She looked at Doña Hilde and shrugged. The señora slapped the long featherstick down in front of me. She spoke to Manuela and left the room.

For once, the cook did not speak crossly. "Doña Hilde hopes a little work will stop you thinking of troubles." But Manuela did not faithfully give me the señora's words. I was beginning to understand Spanish words, and I knew that Doña Hilde had not been so kind.

I took the featherstick and went searching for the highest dust. The cook watched a moment. Then she surprised me. "Leave that. Help me in the kitchen for a while."

Manuela first cooked for the administrator before I was born. Who can count the times she carried meals to the eating table? Who can count the times she wiped spilled coca tea? Always Don Luciano and his family sat talking, and Manuela came to know many *wirajjocha* things. I'd never asked questions because her crossness frightened me.

But Manuela was not mean, and she knew that I wanted to know things. How? Maybe she understood that a daughter thinks and thinks about a faraway father.

She couldn't tell me anything about Father, but she did say things about Bolivia. "It's not a person, Bartolina. It's the *blanco* way of seeing the land."

Instead of *wirajjocha,* she would say *blanco,* a Spanish word that meant *white.*

"When the *blancos* look at the mountains and the Yungas and our high plain, they don't see Kollasuyo. In its place, they find realms named for the biggest towns. La Paz has one, and Masuru belongs to it. Just across the lake, Puno has its realm. Other realms stand with Oruro and Cochabamba, but the *blancos* see farther yet. To the east are wide lowlands, far beyond Kollasuyo. I think the Chaco is there somewhere. Now, all these lands, every single one except Puno, the *blancos* count together as one. They call it Bolivia."

"Bolivia," I repeated. "But what of Puno?"

"They count it among another flock of realms, Peru."

"Manuela, why do they count faraway Chaco lands among Bolivia's realms? Why not take in all of Kollasuyo instead?"

"Who can say? It's the *blanco* way of seeing land."

Then Manuela told me about Salamanca. "You saw those trucks that took the men. They were his."

"He was here? Was Salamanca the man calling out names?"

"No; why should the *presidente* come here? He has the whole of Bolivia to think about."

"*Presidente?*"

"He's head man for all the *blancos.*"

In the hacienda house, Don Luciano's *oficina* was my hardest job. If the administrator left something lying, I couldn't touch it. I had to chase dust around its sides. If he came in, I had to leave—unless his lamp went out. Then I had to stop everything else and go rushing for its tribute. This smelled like a truck and had to be given to the lamp carefully. None could be spilled. When Don Luciano left his *oficina,* I could clean, but I had to use Spanish words to tell Doña Hilde that I was going in. Until I was trusted, she came sitting while I worked.

Mostly she didn't watch me there. She brought something with her, and the way she held it made it look like a huge square hand. Whenever I looked up, she was still sitting there, the whole time looking and looking at this thing. I wondered how long it would take her to see it.

Once Manuela came moaning about trouble in the kitchen. Doña Hilde sighed and followed her out for a look.

She left that thing lying on Don Luciano's working table, open like a flower, but square and white. Woven all through the white were the finest marks of black, like rows of stitches. Seeing them, *I* looked and looked.

Soon I learned that Doña Hilde could *make* those black stitches. To the *oficina* she brought leaves-with-corners, very thin and perfectly white. Sitting at the administrator's table, she dipped a pointed stick into a tiny jar-of-black and wove the blackness into the whiteness. Who hasn't seen a weaver using a pointed llama bone to work the wool? The stick, dancing and dancing in the señora's hand, looked just like that. My strong weaving soul wanted to watch and watch.

Later Grandfather told me about ink and paper. "It's a way of . . . holding words. D'you see?"

I shook my head.

"Think about the señora, then. She comes from Oruro, so her people are far away. When she wants to tell them something, she makes marks for all the words. She doesn't have to go all the way to Oruro to speak them. She just sends the paper with a traveler. Putting the words on paper that way is called *escribiendo*."

Grandfather knew of no Aymara word for *escribiendo*, so I made one: *inkweaving*. "Can you weave the words?"

His smile fled. "Why would I need to? All my people are here."

"I saw Doña Hilde holding many papers woven with ink, all of them clinging together on one edge."

"Books. I've seen them, Bartolina."

"Do they give Doña Hilde news of her family?"

"No. Most were here long before Doña Hilde came."

"What words do they give her?"

Grandfather seemed worried. "Is it our business?"

"She looks and looks. I saw her. What keeps her looking so long?"

Grandfather shrugged. "You shouldn't let it distract you, Bartolina. We have things to keep us occupied, but does Doña Hilde? And how often does anyone visit just for her? Maybe seeing the words is like sitting with a storyteller or a visitor with news."

"The words-on-paper tell news and lore?"

Grandfather heard my excitement, but he only seemed more worried. "It's not something for Masuru people. It's a *wirajjocha* thing. Bartolina, paying too much mind could mean trouble for us Ch'okes."

All I could think about was the inkstick dancing—maybe in *my* hand. "How could it mean trouble?"

"Well, it could." He made his smile return. "We won't speak of it. Then there's no need for worry."

April 1933

Pachamama began giving and giving. Masuru people smiled from the first day they dug for new potatoes. Uncle Jacinto especially smiled.

He came looking at his herd once, just before Adela and I took it to the pasture. "In two months," he said, "I'll help sponsor the feast of Corpus Christi. I can give one of these sheep. I can give *chicha*, too, because I'll have enough of the bitter potatoes to trade for it in Cauquimarca."

I felt proud. "Then you should lead the musicians."

He shrugged. "Maybe yes."

I was sure he would. Uncle had a wide chest that went huge when he played the reed pipes. From the long, low one, he coaxed a song like the lazy brother Wind made tame. I decided happy times would come, and I asked the Virgin of Copacabana to bring Father home quickly so he could share in the feast—or at least the next one after.

Pachamama also gave generously to the *patrón*. With twenty Masuru men still far off, Don Luciano sent the *mayordomos* among the older children to find any strong enough to help with the harvest. Uncle's shouting meant nothing, and Basilia had to leave the pastures.

With Father away, Grandmother had to let her weaving wait. For the first time in many years, she bent over to dig potatoes from our plot. Once I came back from the pasture early to help. She was glad to see me, but still she scolded when she saw me kneeling in the soil. "Mind your skirts unless you want to wear them in shreds. When will we find the time for mending?"

I tried squatting, taking care not to step on my skirts or to catch them with my spade. I'd only dug a few potatoes when I saw Masuru people gathering near Uncle's animal pen.

Among them stood Fortunato Herrán—his big hand holding Dionisio by the neck. My cousin was short, like his father, but not so big in the chest and shoulders. Fortunato stood huge over him. I went running. Uncle had been digging in his own plot, and he went running, too.

Fortunato called to Uncle, even while he was still coming. "Jacinto, you'll want to know what I saw today."

Dionisio's face was bruised and bloody. He held his arms tight across his chest. He wouldn't let himself cry out, but I could see tears on his cheek. Uncle showed a soul of rage.

The *mayordomo* pretended not to see. "This lazy boy of yours would rather disobey Don Luciano than work his share."

"Fortunato, let Dionisio loose. He owes no service."

"Do you think that potatoes won't rot in the fields just because men are away? I took old Cipriano from the stable to help with the harvest. I needed Dionisio to take over the feeding of the administrator's horses. But, Jacinto, I had the hardest time finding him."

"Dionisio," Uncle said, "go in the house."

My cousin began to move, but Fortunato pulled him back, still clutching his neck.

"Your boy has been seeing that Baptist. I saw him coming out myself. I think he needs a beating, Jacinto."

Uncle's voice was low and fierce. "Maybe he's already had one from someone who is not his father."

Aunt Cristina dropped a bundle of *totora* reeds she was bringing from market. She pushed past everyone and ran toward her son. Fortunato's big hand met her shoulder and knocked her back.

I never saw Uncle move so fast. Fortunato had only one instant to let go of Dionisio and reach for his whip. He was too slow. Uncle's strong shoulder struck him low and drove him down. A moment later, Uncle was standing. He pulled Fortunato up by the shirt. He lifted the *mayordomo* right off the ground like a big sack of coca, and again Fortunato thumped down hard.

He had to crawl away. When he was almost to the road, he finally stood and began limping toward the hacienda house.

People and people came looking to see what would happen next. One was Grandfather. He'd been mending the *patrón*'s pasture wall but came hurrying when he saw the fight.

Everyone knew Fortunato would return. It was no surprise that he didn't come alone. From horseback, Don Luciano himself called for Uncle to appear. Two other *mayordomos* seized him when he did. There were cries— Aunt's and mine together—when Fortunato struck him. He struck again to the belt, then finally to the chin.

Uncle fell bleeding. The two other *mayordomos* stood back, and Fortunato raised his whip. Everyone jumped clear except Grandfather. "There's been enough trouble. Dionisio won't be going back to the Baptist, I'll promise—"

The whip bit his hands and face and neck. I screamed, but not Grandfather.

"Don Luciano, please!" he appealed. His obliging voice pleaded higher and faster than I'd ever heard. "What's done is done. Jacinto and the boy have taken their punishment. They understand about the Baptist now."

"Stand aside, Alfonso," said the administrator, and a *may-ordomo* pulled Grandfather away.

"Jacinto," said Fortunato, "that Baptist speaks against Padre Roberto." He brought the whip down. Uncle's eyes squeezed tightly shut. "Jacinto, are you listening? The *patrón* doesn't allow Masuru people to hear slander."

The whip fell twice more. I felt myself shaking. Tears fell down my cheeks. I thought I should intervene against the whip the way Grandfather had. I felt ashamed for being too frightened. I wished that the Baptist had never come. I wished that Dionisio had stayed minding sheep.

Fortunato drew the whip back for another strike. "Enough!" called Don Luciano. He stepped down from his horse and untied the gate to Uncle's animal pen. With everyone watching, he pulled a knife from his belt and cut away the red and green threads from the big alpaca's ear. His heavy boot ground the Ch'oke earmark into the soil. Then he led Uncle's animal to the gate. "Fortunato, here's something for your trouble." He called to the other two *mayordomos*. "There's a sheep here for each of you."

Uncle lay in the dust, his breath coming quickly. Aunt knelt over him, crying. The widow Concevida brought a basket of curing leaves. Through bloody tears in Uncle's shirt, Aunt laid the leaves over the whip bites. Other women began tending to Dionisio and Grandfather.

Uncle finally opened his eyes—and saw Don Luciano's boot close to his face. "It's a busy time for all of us, Jacinto." The administrator didn't speak fiercely. He might have been telling Doña Hilde to give him sugar for tea. "Send your boy to my stable tomorrow. I need him there."

The next day, I went early to my service. Passing the stable, I looked for Dionisio but didn't see him. I had to help Manuela carry her own water because Grandfather didn't come. That scared me, but there was no time to go looking for anyone. By the time we had enough water, mules arrived carrying rolls of matting.

Doña Hilde thought the floor in the hacienda house was too cold. Her feet hid in shoes tied tightly around them, so why did she care? Still, she wanted matting. Two men had to be called away from the harvest to move everything. Then they rolled long matting strips onto the floor. I spent most of the day sewing them together. When the sun went low, Doña Hilde came looking and sighed. "It will have to do."

Coming home, I was near Father's door when I heard Grandfather inside. "I begged them!"

Why was he at our house, not Uncle's? But he kept speaking, and I quickly forgot that question. Never had I heard such weeping in Grandfather's voice. " 'You still have some sheep,' I said. 'You can manage here. Why risk everything?' It was no good. What will happen to them now?"

I pushed past the blanket that hung over the door. "Grandfather?"

He only moaned.

My eyes found Grandmother's. "Your Uncle Jacinto and his family went to their plot under the moon last night. They worked and worked until they had all the potatoes they could carry. With the first sun, they took their sheep and followed the stream that passes Huarina."

"But Dionisio had service in the stable. Don Luciano will be angry."

Grandmother spoke in a low, calm voice. "Bartolina, they've left the Ch'oke lands."

"Maybe Dionisio still ached from the beating. That's what I'll tell—"

"Bartolina!" Grandmother's shout hushed me. "You don't have to make any excuse for your cousin. A *mayordomo* saw them go. Don Luciano already knows they've quit Masuru."

My eyes went wide. Uncle and Aunt had lived on the hacienda all their lives. When hadn't Basilia and Dionisio been near? Adela was my best friend! I almost yelled at Grandmother. "Where can they live but here?"

Grandfather moaned. "I asked Jacinto the same thing. He said they can reach La Paz."

I looked to Grandmother.

"He wanted you to go," she said. Her voice was calm, but I could still hear its great anger—at Uncle. "He wanted all of us to go. I told him our people's lives are here. Donato will return here. We honor dead who are buried *here*."

Grandfather shook his head. "At the planting, I begged Jacinto not to send Dionisio to that Baptist. Later I begged him to stop sending the boy."

"Why send him at all?" I asked. "Why hear words against Padre Roberto?"

"It wasn't the spoken words, Bartolina. That Baptist knows the words-on-paper. Jacinto wanted Dionisio to learn them, too. Remember, Bartolina? I told you they could be trouble. I told Jacinto the same thing—again and again. Why didn't he listen? He and Donato never needed words-on-paper."

"Grandfather, when will we see them?"

"Will we ever? We won't know where they're living. We won't know *if* they're living. Maybe they'll lose the way. Maybe they'll meet thieves or the lazy brother Frost along the road." I'd never heard Grandfather speak so fearfully. "Even if they manage for now, those potatoes and sheep can only feed them so long. They'll run out of food. *What then?*"

April–May 1933

Don Luciano would never allow one old man alone to hold a house and plot, so Grandfather came to live with us in Father's house. That was easy to settle, but other things were not.

I still had my service *and* Father's sheep. The morning after my cousins left, I asked Grandfather how I could manage both. Since it was my herding day, he sent me to the pasture as usual. When I came back, he had an answer.

"A new family came to Masuru just before the planting, people that Donato liked. Well, the man was sent off to the Chaco, but I spoke to the woman today. Her daughter can watch our sheep during your service. You'll tend their sheep on days that the girl weaves or helps with marketing."

"What girl?" Grandmother asked.

"Simona Páez."

I went stiff. My cousin Basilia had warned me about Simona Páez.

Grandmother answered sharply. "Simona is a twin! Did her mother tell you that?"

"Juana Páez didn't have to tell me. That talk has been all over. It didn't bother Donato. Why should we worry?"

I *did* worry. Twins born at Masuru always meant hardship and sometimes worse. Often one twin came dead. Sometimes one came feet first or made the mother bleed until she died. Those incorrect births were especially frightening to all Masuru. Sometimes they brought fierce, cold, incorrect rains—the lazy brother Hail. Grandfather's agreement surprised me because everyone knew that bad luck swirled around twins.

"How long before a sheep is lost?" Grandmother asked him. "How long before another falls to a fox? What chance is there that we'll have a single animal left by the feast of Saint Peter?"

"Didn't I just say that Donato respected this family? We'll have our sheep, Julia."

"Will we? When has a twin ever come to any good?"

At first Grandfather went silent. Maybe he worried, too. Finally he shrugged. "What good comes by letting sheep watch themselves? Will you go into the pasture with them?"

"I am old. Must I walk to the far pasture? How can I chase after lambs when a fox comes near?"

"There you have it," said Grandfather. "Simona Páez will help Bartolina with our sheep."

Juana Páez and her twin daughter lived in one of the houses just to our side of the *patrón*'s stables. The other twin was dead, but Grandmother warned me just the same. "Don't believe anyone telling you that Simona isn't still a twin."

I went warily the next morning and found Simona waiting. She stood smaller than me, but I wasn't fooled. I knew from Masuru talk that she was my same age.

"I have six sheep," I told her. "I've been watching them closely—every single one. I marked their ears with my father's special knot." I spoke this so she'd see that I couldn't be tricked. If she brought back only five sheep, I would know. If she changed an earmark and gave me back a sick, thin ewe for a hearty one, I would know.

"I'll bring them here just before dark, Bartolina." Her eyes wouldn't hold mine. The whole time, she held her chin low and tugged at one of her braids.

"That's when I'll come for my six sheep."

Soon after, I met Fortunato Herrán at the hacienda house. His eyes found me, and I put *my* chin low. He stood in the gateway so that I couldn't pass. I wondered if he would scold—or worse—because he knew I was cousin to Dionisio.

"I don't know if it's true," he said. I didn't hear the least sound of anger. "But you'd better mind, just in case."

"Mind what?"

"They're saying there's a condor, a purely wicked one." He kept speaking, but with no more than a whisper. "They're saying he eats children. Now it's a shame to worry you, but what if it's true? What then?"

I thought of my cousins wandering somewhere beneath the wide sky. "What children did he eat?"

The *mayordomo* shrugged. "Any he was able to trick, I suppose. You should watch out. I heard he caught a boy at Escoma. They're saying the boy was nothing but bones when that condor finished. They're saying he ate a boy *and* a girl at Pucarani. He offers to tell all sorts of things, then ..." Fortunato just shook his head.

"This condor speaks?"

"He appears as a man. D'you see? That's why he's so dangerous. I can keep watch, but if he seems to be just a man, how will I know him?" I'd never seen Fortunato tremble, but he did just then. "Bartolina, have you ever seen a condor use his beak?"

I remembered the one who had swept close that time— red comb and white collar, naked neck, huge black wings. I thought of his savage talons and beak.

"Bartolina, if you see anyone strange, be wary. If anyone

wants to tell you things that are none of your business, watch out. Our *patrón* only wants what's best for people on his land. Think how he'd suffer if some Masuru girl were ripped to bits. I'm telling you as a favor to him: Fear the condor."

He walked off without another word.

If something had happened in Cauquimarca, Masuru people would know. But who could say about Escoma or Pucarani? We didn't know the families there. I went into the house and made Doña Hilde's eating table shine with polish, but all day I thought and thought about that condor.

Later Simona came back with the sheep, all of them, all the right ones. Grandmother and Grandfather came hurrying as soon as they heard me putting them into our pen. Both looked closely at the sheep.

I had worried, too, but more about another thing. "Fortunato Herrán said—"

"Aaai! He's a fox!" shouted Grandmother.

"Julia," warned Grandfather, "you'll be heard."

Grandmother wasn't finished. "I want to spit when I hear his name!"

I didn't want her spitting. I didn't want her shouting anything that might bring trouble. So I waited until later before asking again. And then I didn't say Fortunato's name. I only asked if a condor might appear as a man.

"I've heard of it in stories," Grandmother said, "but I've never seen it."

"Still, it's always best to stay clear of strange people," said Grandfather. "Why take risks?"

Whenever I left my animals with Simona, it was the same. None was ever lost. Maybe, I thought, bad luck hides and waits. I was especially careful on the days that I looked after

Simona's sheep. I worried about provoking her, and Grandmother warned me more than once: "Don't get her angry."

When I saw Simona mornings and evenings, we would just say a few words. Her eyes never found mine. Soon I knew her sheep better than I knew her. Why not? I tended the sheep all day. I learned which lamb always stayed close to its mother. I knew each sheep's voice—even well enough to know if it sensed danger or just bleated foolishness.

Yet I didn't know everything. Were sheep bad luck because a twin stood over them? And what of the wicked condor? Should I watch for someone flying or someone walking? With Basilia far away, I had to depend even more on my brother. I prayed and prayed, always asking Casimiro to keep alert.

Sometimes, maybe one day each week, Simona and I both went to the pastures. I remembered what Grandmother had said, and I was glad that Simona didn't ask to herd with me.

Then, a few days before the feast of the Holy Cross, I saw that she'd brought her flock quite close to mine. We stood among the lowest hills just into the far pasture. It seemed strange that we'd come so far only to find ourselves standing so close. I took my sheep a little farther away.

Simona moved her flock a few steps closer again, and I began to worry. With a step now and a step then, she brought her flock even closer. One of my souls said to move away quickly, but another said moving away might anger Simona.

I was trying to choose when I heard a bell. It rang and rang from somewhere nearby, but hidden among the hills. At first I stood wary, but then a large llama, his head high and the bell at his chest, appeared from between hills. He passed close enough that I could see red and green tassels hanging from his ears. Coming into the pasture, he never looked to one side or the other. The whole time he knew just where he was, and just where he was going—toward Achacachi.

Four men, a boy, and twenty more llamas followed that proud leader into the pasture. They'd come through the mountain passes from the Yungas. The llamas carried sacks and baskets full of fruits, spices, and coca. When they stopped to rest, I wanted to run and see, but I had to mind. A pair of foxes might appear quickly. Besides, I didn't know the men. Who might be standing among them?

Suddenly Simona was speaking almost beside me. "Do they come from Canocaya or Para Para?" she asked, all the time looking at the train, never at me.

Why ask me about faraway places? "Maybe Canocaya," I answered.

"No one's collecting the droppings."

I watched, and Simona was right. Most of those animals left piles of the small pellets that llamas drop. No one took them up. Soon the bell began to ring again, and the train moved on. "I'll watch your sheep," said Simona. "You go collecting. Don't you need some?"

It was true. The droppings could be mixed with potato ash and given as tribute to Pachamama before the next planting. Or they could be dried and mixed with *yareta* to feed a cook fire. "You'll need some, too," I said. "We'll share."

Simona shook her head. "You go. Next time a train comes through, you watch our sheep and I'll collect."

I took my *yareta* sack toward the droppings, but still I worried. Each of us could have moved her flock and collected without the other's help. Maybe Simona wanted to steal my sheep. But if she did, wouldn't she do it on a day when she was minding them with me away?

All my sheep were safe when I returned.

Later Grandfather smiled when he saw the droppings I'd collected. I told him about the train and about Simona.

"You should have shared anyway, Bartolina. Simona and her mother don't have much. Next time a train comes through, see that she takes all the droppings. After that, share evenly."

Grandmother heard him. "Does this mean Bartolina now herds with that Simona?"

Grandfather pretended not to hear the anger in her voice. "Simona's family isn't a bad one. Didn't I tell you? Before he went off to the Chaco, Evaristo Páez said he wanted to help sponsor a feast as soon as he could. That's something coming from a new man with only four sheep."

Grandmother never spoke against these words. But the next time we wove together, she reminded me that Simona was a twin. "Who is your best friend, Bartolina?" she asked, her hardest eyes finding me.

I was silent for a moment, then spoke sadly, "My cousin Adela."

May 1933

O n her next weaving day, Simona came to leave her
sheep. I saw her looking past me, and just then I
heard something. The sky was too clear for thunder.

I looked south and saw dust fleeing from the road. My
first thought was of Father, but the coming truck was black,
not green. I remembered the danger to sheep, and I ran
hard. I shooed every single sheep well back.

I hoped the truck would stop where the southern stream
flowed across the road, but even that didn't worry it. It
bellowed through the water. It never stopped to make an
offering to the stream's grandfather.

Men and women from the nearest houses gathered.
Grandfather came looking among them, and I worried that
he was standing too close to the road. I grew fearful when
the truck stopped right beside him. It was the one I'd seen
outside the Baptist mission in Cauquimarca.

When the Baptist stepped out and faced the sun, I went
stiff. I'd never seen him from so close. The shoulder of his
black coat reached as high as my tall grandfather's head. A
bit of white collar reached even higher. But above that . . .

Who hasn't seen a potato cut open? The inside is almost
as white as the cap of Illampu. So was the Baptist's face and

long, naked neck! He didn't have a trace of brownness to him. His hair frightened me even more.

It was red.

"A wonderful thing happened!" called the Baptist. "I've come to tell you." He spoke the Aymara words, yet he made them sound so strange.

The Baptist held a book in front of him. "The *One* Grandfather of all the world and sky loves and loves and loves us—so much that he sent his only son. All who let their eyes see Jesus will have safe souls forever."

"Grandfather, please!" This was *my* grandfather, calling to the Baptist.

"Alfonso, it's my joy to see you again. But call me Brother."

"And I greet you, Grand—"

The Baptist's eyes seemed to scold.

"I greet you, Brother," said Grandfather. "But it's not good that you come to the hacienda. It's not allowed without the administrator's permission. There's sure to be trouble if Don Luciano sees you." Then he told the Baptist about Dionisio, about all the trouble.

"I'm sorry for that. I'd hoped I might see him here." The Baptist went quiet for a moment. He looked down at his book and pushed and pushed at its leaves. Then his eyes met Grandfather's again. "Dionisio looked upon this book. He repeated these words, spoken in far-past times by the one who saves us: 'Those punished for chasing correctness are favored. The One Grandfather's realm is theirs.' Alfonso, take comfort that Jesus is with Dionisio wherever he is."

"Listen, Grandfather. I'll tell everyone here about Jesus. We spoke on the first day Dionisio went to you. Remember?" My grandfather began using his obliging voice. "There's no sense looking for trouble. If you turn your truck, you can go right out the way you came. The administrator won't see."

The Baptist put a hand on Grandfather's shoulder. "Brother, did we talk for even an hour? There's so much more to tell."

"Please!" pleaded Grandfather.

The Baptist turned to the rest of us. He said he wanted us to go to his place in Cauquimarca and to hear his words. Everyone should come, he said—men, women, the smallest of children. I listened, still worried about the strangeness he gave to familiar words. And there was something more about him. My fearing soul screamed a warning—but about what?

Then everyone began shouting and pointing. Don Luciano had just ridden from the stable.

"Get in your truck," begged Grandfather. "Go back quickly. He won't follow you past the stream."

The Baptist never moved. Don Luciano's rifle hung over his back. When he arrived, sitting high on horseback, even the Baptist had to look up at him. Not one person watching spoke a word. They all saw the whip tied to the saddle.

"This is private land," said Don Luciano. I listened hard because he used the Spanish words. "Get back in your truck. You cannot stop here."

The Baptist held his hand toward Don Luciano. "I am—"

"I know you. You are the Canadian Baptist, but these are Catholic lands."

"I come in friendship."

"Then why do you sneak in from the south? The shortest road from Cauquimarca is that way, past my house."

"I travel openly. My work took me to Pucarani yesterday, so I'm coming from the south this morning."

"I'm sure that's very likely, but you have no work here."

"Father, my work isn't done until everyone has heard the words of Jesus."

I was surprised. *Father* is respectful, but no one ever spoke that word to the administrator. He wanted a Spanish word—*señor* or *don*. Then I realized that all the Baptist's speaking had stayed with the Aymara words. He kept using them with Don Luciano—and loudly enough for everyone to hear. "You're as welcome at my mission as anyone. Bring your sons, your wife—"

"Enough!" shouted the administrator. He looked at all of us, and for a small moment I thought that he would shoo us away. Instead, he looked back to the Baptist—and started using the Aymara words himself. "Our *patrón* provides for these people's souls. He sends a proper priest, Padre Roberto, to make certain that every single one is secure within the true faith. There's no place for a foreign sect here. And I caution you, the *patrón* has given me exact instructions concerning trespassers."

We all took in every last word spoken between the Baptist and the administrator. No one else made a sound.

"Where is this Padre Roberto?" asked the Baptist. "How many babies have died unbaptized since he last came?"

"Padre Roberto is a man of the *true* faith." Don Luciano's eyes held the Baptist, but his hands loosened the whip from its ties.

The Baptist spread his arms—so wide. His black coat hung open, and my fearing soul stirred again, as if it recognized him. "Do our brothers and sisters here understand the Latin Mass? Does Padre Roberto repeat after Jesus using their own Aymara words?"

"He serves us well!" Then Don Luciano went back to his Spanish words. "Now, I have told you before. Take your truck and leave Masuru."

The Baptist looked to his book and spoke out to all of us. "Here I have the speaking of Jesus."

"I warn you, Señor!"

"Do you deny these people salvation?"

The administrator lashed out. The Masuru people standing closest leaped back. The Baptist swung his arm high to meet the whip. His fingers—long and spread wide—looked like huge feathers at the tip of a great wing.

My fearing soul cried a new warning. *D'you see the disguise?* I heard a scream—mine. I knew that black garment, naked neck, and red crown!

I ran many steps before remembering my sheep. I turned and saw the Baptist, blood showing through a torn sleeve, still facing Don Luciano. I waited for him to transform and fly at the administrator. I waited for him to send his truck raging against the horse.

But the battle had already ended. The Baptist only spoke, again with Aymara words. "Paul took pleasure from the suffering that came to him for speaking of Jesus."

He began stepping backward. He opened his truck door, but then once more he spoke to the Masuru people. "My place in Cauquimarca is open to you all. Let Jesus stand with you, and remember his words: 'Pray for those who harass you.' " The Baptist gave one last look toward Don Luciano; then he banged his truck door shut.

Out with my sheep that day, I kept watch for the Baptist every single moment. I searched road, pasture, and sky.

June–July 1933

F inally, mules and llamas carried the *patrón*'s last crops toward La Paz. Masuru people forgot the harvest labors and gathered in the near pasture for the feast of Corpus Christi.

My grandparents and I watched the spear dance. Twenty-six Masuru men circled to the drum's call. They blew shrill whistles while two more in kilts of jaguar fur spun their long spears inside the circle. Everyone watching shouted and laughed whenever one took a wrong step. D'you see? It was a contest between the two in the center. Each man tried to make the other step badly.

I told Grandfather, "You should be in the center twirling a spear."

He laughed. I was glad to hear it because Grandfather's joyous smiles had hidden since Uncle went away. "You must think that I'm very brave."

Only Grandmother seemed cross. "Do you think those two are brave? Their grandfathers would have laughed at them."

I thought of Father. He was brave. He was the one I truly wanted to see in the spear dance. Worries came sneaking past the musicians, troubling my souls over news I'd heard from the market women. One said that the Guaraní killed fifty of our men as they pushed into some new part of the Chaco. I asked, "What are the names of the men killed?" The market woman didn't know. More and more news told of men being killed.

Right there, with the feast going on around me, I whispered to my *angelito*. "Casimiro, I'll ask the Virgin of Copacabana to protect me from the condor. I'll give the grandfather of Illampu a special offering to watch over me. I'll be safe, little brother."

I sat frightened, wondering if I believed my own words. Still, I had to finish my prayer. "Casimiro, someone needs your intervention more than me. Go to the Chaco! Protect our father. Watch over him every single moment until he's safe."

What more could I do? The songs of the short reed pipes made my weaving soul think of quick, tiny hands working and working the wool. Even my fearing soul calmed itself a bit.

Since the llama train came through, Simona and I had herded together once each week. We hid ourselves among the hills of the far pasture so that Grandmother couldn't see.

I always gave an offering for the grandfather of Illampu. I remembered Basilia's trick against danger, and we kept our sheep close and moving often. I watched and watched, especially in the sky, but I trembled less with Simona looking, too. If we sat facing each other, we didn't need to keep turning and turning like one person alone.

Once we took wool cord, tied its ends, and wove figures between our fingers. Simona showed me *Seven Eyes,* and I showed her *Spider.* Another time she asked me about someone who worried her.

"There's a girl in Cauquimarca, maybe our age, Bartolina. But she never speaks. If a boy comes teasing, she just shrieks and runs to her mother."

"Soledad Girón," I said.

"If she sees a llama staring at her, she moans and wails. She pulls and pulls at her mother's sleeve. That poor mother!"

I explained just as Grandmother had once explained to me. "That mother was unwise. Soledad got sick when she was tiny. Her mother took her to a curer, but they crossed a stream getting to him."

"The stream's grandfather took one of Soledad's souls?"

"Maybe two, one each way. Maybe the soul of a drowned fisherman came wandering along that stream and stole another. The curer tried calling back her lost souls, but it was no good. Grandmother says that Soledad has just one soul left, and it never speaks."

Later we talked a long time about families, Simona's and mine. I told her something I'd never told anyone. I said I couldn't remember my mother's face. "When I think of her, I see only my cousin Basilia's face."

"I have one that I lost long ago," she said. "My brother Ignacio died when we—when he was small." She looked away. She didn't want to remind me of what everyone knew. "He died even before his first haircutting."

Yet she looked back quickly. More and more she let her eyes hold mine.

We usually met at Chuyma, the low hill in the near pasture, before going to the far pasture. Once I went early, right to the top of the hill. I sat without moving—except for my eyes. Away and back, away and back, they searched along the road. Soon Simona brought her sheep and looked with me. "They've been gone a long time, Bartolina. Mother didn't want Father to serve those trucks. She said we should flee to her people near Huarina, but he didn't want to depend on her people."

My father had not been the only one called, yet I hadn't

thought a single moment about the other men. I only remembered Evaristo Páez when Simona spoke.

"Grandmother didn't want my father to go either." I told her the things my grandparents had said, except for the words about the cave beneath Iquiña.

"Why do our fathers have to serve that Salamanca, Bartolina? What does Salamanca give in return?"

I had no answer.

All that day we let our sheep graze around Chuyma while we watched the road. At first we led them to the top. When they chewed that grass low, I moved them to one side, then to another. Mostly, we didn't stand among them. We wanted to be right at the top of the hill. Maybe we had to chase a lamb wandering too far, but when it settled again, we went back to the highest spot.

How could Grandmother not see? That evening she and I set our weaving frames just outside our house. Grandfather sat with pipes, the kind with five reeds tied together, each with its own note. I chanted softly with him. My weaving soul was especially happy since I was working a whole train of llamas into a shawl—not for the *patrón,* but for me.

But after a time, Grandmother raised her hand, and Grandfather put down his pipes. "Bartolina," she said, "you went herding the whole day with that Simona Páez."

"That's Grandfather's arrangement."

"No! He said you could care for each other's sheep when there is the need, not stand together when there isn't. She's a twin. Don't you know what bad luck that can mean?"

"She isn't mad at me. Why should I worry about her?"

Grandfather spoke. Maybe he had grown tired of facing Grandmother's fiercest eyes. "How can you be sure about such things, Bartolina? Isn't it best to be safe?"

"I *am* safe with Simona."

"Bartolina!" shouted Grandmother. "Respect your grand-father."

The next time Simona and I herded together, I decided, I would say that our sheep needed to spread out more. I would say we should stand apart to watch them better.

But on that day, Simona came crying to Chuyma. She began telling me about a market woman who said that the men wouldn't be back even for the next planting. "Barto-lina, there are uncountable thousands of Guaraní in the Chaco. They won't let themselves be pushed out."

She repeated all the market talk. Men in the Chaco would stay, except for those wounded or killed, until the Guaraní were beaten. No one would be excused. Those men might be gone all through the next green season.

I didn't leave Simona alone that day. Why would I when she was so upset? But I must say the truth. *I* didn't want to be alone after hearing still more talk about men being killed.

The next week, I herded with Simona again. I thought I'd surely hear Grandmother's harshest tongue that night. I thought of things to shout back. She *did* speak to me, but her words were soft. "You told me once that Adela Ch'oke was your best friend. What do you tell me now?"

I didn't want to lie. I said nothing.

"Why do you disobey when I ask you to be careful around this Simona Páez?"

"She is not a bad person, Grandmother. I know it!"

"Bartolina, I have only said that she is a twin."

"She would never send bad luck to me."

"Sometimes bad luck is not sent. I think this is especially the way with a young twin. Even if Simona is completely innocent, bad luck follows her. It finds those who go near."

"Should I still choose Adela as my best friend? I never scc hcr. I don't know what happencd to her."

Grandmother sighed. We wove silently for a time, but I knew she would speak again. Even so, she surprised me. "Do you remember little Casimiro?"

Why talk about my brother? "I remember."

"Remember how weak your mother was after he was born? For nearly a year, she grew thinner and thinner. At the end she hardly spoke, and then she died."

My fearing soul listened to every word.

"I wasn't going to frighten you, but now I must speak." Grandmother barely whispered the next thing. "I know the power of twins because Casimiro was a twin."

"No! I remember. I never saw two babies."

"Where were you when he came?"

"Right here. I remember how tiny he looked."

"Where were you the very moment he was born?"

I thought a moment. "You sent me away—to Uncle's house."

"Bartolina, the first bad luck came to the little sister in the womb with Casimiro. She never took a breath and was never named. I cremated her on a slope of Iquiña. I did it quickly so that no one would call Casimiro a twin."

"But he died *before* Mother. How could he cause her death? And he'd never do it. He's completely innocent! He sits with the saints."

"Bartolina, why don't you listen? Casimiro didn't send out the evil, but it swarmed around him. It probably caused his own death, but even before that, it found your mother. I know it, girl! It all happened before my eyes."

July–August 1933

I didn't tell Simona what Grandmother had said. On the next day that we both went to the pasture, I took my sheep out very early. I drove them past Chuyma toward the far pasture and found a new spot among Illampu's toes north of Iquiña. Simona didn't find me.

Grandmother went asking all around Masuru and found what she wanted. "Do you know that boy Raúl?" she said when I returned. "He's nine years old and from a good family. They say he's responsible. When you do your service at the house, you can leave your sheep with him."

"What of Grandfather's arrangement?"

"I saw Juana Páez today. I thanked her for Simona's help, but I told her it will no longer be needed."

"Who'll watch Simona's sheep when she weaves with her mother?"

"I don't know the answer, Bartolina, but Simona managed before you watched her flock. She'll manage again."

Weeks later, in Cauquimarca, I went looking at a row of wide tin pots shining in the sun. Simona came to see at the very same moment that I finished. I turned, and just in that instant we stood facing each other. I tried to think of words, but Simona turned away.

I was relieved, but later two of my souls made war against each other. My weaving soul remembered the times Simona and I made yarn figures, the times we watched for our fathers. It longed to respect Grandfather's broken agreement, but my fearing soul had listened to Grandmother. It found strength from her.

Once, sitting by the cook fire, I let my fingers make *Seven Eyes*. Right away I felt tears, and Grandmother saw them. "Why are you crying?"

"Because it's never any good trying to have a best friend."

"I'm sorry, Bartolina, but a best friend can bring misfortune if she's a twin. It can come in many different ways. This is one way, and just be glad that it isn't worse. Think about your weaving or herding, and soon you'll forget that Simona."

Grandmother's wisdom seemed great. For a moment I even wondered if Father should have followed her words and gone hiding in that cave. I didn't know. I only worried. I heard more news from market women in Cauquimarca. One spoke of a new killing place in the Chaco—Nanawa.

Again I asked, "What are the names of the men killed?"

The woman shook her head. "I don't know the names, but if I did, the sun would be gone before I could say them all."

Again and again, I asked the Virgin of Copacabana to intervene against the Guaraní. I heard others praying to her, but I feared that the Chaco was beyond her influence.

I thought and thought about Casimiro. Did the bad luck fall away when he went to sit among the saints? Or had I sent it along with him—straight to Father?

The ice season neared its end, and Masuru men began plowing to prepare for the next planting. Salamanca's trucks came again while Grandmother and I stood in Cauquimarca's market square. They bellowed right past us.

I shouted Father's name, but the trucks didn't stop. They rushed on toward Masuru. Poles and tight cloth made tents over their pens. I tried to look into the back, but black shadows wouldn't let me see. I found Grandmother's eyes, and she knew my question before I asked it. "Go and see," she said. "I'll manage here."

I ran hard until I passed the cemetery, but my lungs burned and I had to walk a little way. Finally I went running the rest of the way, but not so fast.

Many Masuru people already stood around the gate of the hacienda house, where the trucks had stopped. By the time I reached them, I could see that no one was happy. Don Luciano stood looking especially unhappy. Beside him a soldier was reading names from a list. Coming nearer, I heard the last one he called: Fortunato Herrán. Everyone began talking. After Nanawa, Salamanca needed more men.

I asked Manuela, "Have they brought back the men who've already served?"

"Just Guillermo Quispe. He's in the middle of that bunch. Everyone's trying to hear him."

I couldn't get near, so I watched the administrator. Don Luciano held a hand on Fortunato's shoulder. He shook his other hand at the soldier. "All four of my *mayordomos* are on your list. You leave me with boys and old men. Let me keep this one man for the planting."

"Señor, these are times of war, times of sacrifice."

"No one can say I'm not doing my share. I have two sons in officer training."

"I'm sorry, Señor. I have my orders."

Who had ever seen Don Luciano defeated? He never even reached for his whip or rifle.

I turned and almost yelled out. Guillermo Quispe finally stood clear, and I could see all of him at once. Deep wounds twisted one side of his face. Strips of cloth around his head held a little cover over his eye. Or maybe he'd left that eye in the Chaco. On the same side a long stick reached from the ground up under his arm. He needed it because most of his leg had stayed in the Chaco, too.

He saw me. "What are you staring at, girl?"

I wanted to run, but I had to ask. "Father Guillermo, please! What about Donato Ch'oke?"

"Bartolina?" I nodded, and he forgot his fierceness. "Your father and I were in the same troop the whole time since leaving Masuru. I last saw him soon before an attack on the Guaraní fort at Nanawa. He was fine then—not a thing wrong with him. But then I went scouting. I put my nose in the wrong place. Well, you can see what happened. I had to come away. I can't say what happened to Donato at Nanawa."

Again I had thought only of *my* father. I'm ashamed because Guillermo knew everything about Evaristo Páez. He could have told me right then, but I didn't ask.

Two days after the trucks had taken fifty more Masuru men, I came home from my service at the hacienda house. Grandmother was weaving just outside our door. Grandfather was shaping a basin from clay, something he hadn't done for many years. He looked worried. "How will we manage the planting, Julia?"

"Our young men are sent to faraway service. The *patrón* cannot expect his fields to be planted."

"You know what Don Luciano says, Julia. It's wartime. Everyone has to do a little extra."

"Extra? One Masuru man now walks with a stick. Three more are dead!"

That surprised me. "Who?"

Grandfather named two Masuru men who had died with fever in the Chaco. "And it's such a shame—Evaristo Páez fell at Nanawa. Guillermo brought Juana stones from his grave."

The next morning my weaving soul pushed away my fearing soul. As soon as the awakening sky chased most of the darkness, I ran out of my house. Grandfather had said that Juana and Simona would go back to their people near Huarina that same morning. When I found their house and sheep pen already empty, I wept.

Still, I knew that Simona and Juana would be dragging sleeping mats. They'd be carrying their things and driving sheep all at once. A moment later I was running. I passed the hacienda house and turned toward town. I saw them ahead, with pots and blankets on their backs and baskets tied to their belts.

"Simona!" I called when I was near enough.

She and her mother turned, but Simona turned right back toward Cauquimarca. She kept walking.

"I'm so sorry about your father," I said. "I will say many prayers."

Juana called after her daughter. "Your best friend says she has prayers for Father."

Simona turned—just to her mother. She never looked at me. "That Bartolina better watch out! She's standing awfully close. Who knows what awful luck she'll have." Again she was walking away.

Juana turned to me. "Let me say something to her."

I didn't wait. Anger seized me, too, and I ran all the way to where my sheep waited. But by the time I reached the pen, I only felt sorrow. My tears fell for the second time that day, and the sun had not yet climbed above the mountains.

September 1933–March 1934

A month after Fortunato and the others rode toward the Chaco, we rested to remember the birth of the Virgin. Don Luciano himself sponsored the feast of the Nativity. He gave coca and *chicha* to the old men. He gave hard sweets to everyone. Then he pointed toward the *patrón*'s fields. "Much less than usual will be planted. The *patrón* knows these are difficult times. He wants to set an example of the sacrifice we all must make."

The next day we learned that he intended to sacrifice only a quarter of the crop. The rest, the administrator said, must be planted. With the strongest men away, the older men had to return to plowing. Even a few women walked behind the *patrón*'s oxen, guiding plows.

Children, women carrying the unborn, and the oldest men followed the plows. I was called and followed among them. I swung and swung and swung the stone head of a clod crusher. My hands ached and bled, even before the first day ended. Soon they weren't so nimble, and I could hardly weave. But why worry? With service in the fields *and* hacienda house, when could I? If I did, when would I sleep?

I never went to the pastures. That boy Raúl looked after my sheep every day, and his mother said we would have to give one sheep for all his help. I thought Grandmother would be mad, and she was—but not at Raúl's mother.

Don Luciano said I would work in the house a day and a morning each week, not three days. Doña Hilde wasn't happy. She wailed about how quickly dust came sneaking. Don Luciano explained that the planting had to be first, but as soon as he went riding, she moaned again. Sometimes when I went to work just the morning, she wouldn't excuse me until part of the afternoon was gone.

Grandfather's slow step wouldn't do during the planting. Each morning he hurried to bring six buckets of water to the hacienda house. If Manuela or the family needed more, Manuela herself had to carry it because Grandfather spent the rest of the day serving as a *mayordomo* in the fields.

Grandmother had not gone to the *patrón*'s fields for many seasons, and she still did not go. Soon I saw that she had stopped all her weaving for the *patrón*. That frightened me. "Maybe Don Luciano will come with a whip. What then?"

"Bartolina, you've seen me weaving late into the night. I make clothes for many Masuru people who are so burdened with service that they can't weave. I work because they still need protection against the lazy brother Frost."

I hadn't seen until that moment how weary she was.

"Girl, the administrator knows that shivering people are no good in the fields. He knows that I *am* serving the *patrón*." These last words held anger—quiet but great.

When the soil was ready, the seeds still had to be put down. The broad bean planting came first. Grandfather told me what to do. "Drive a hole with your measuring stick, then drop a seed and press a little mound over it. Measure the distance for the next hole with the stick, then repeat. When you get to the end of the row, you can rest until everyone finishes. Then everyone together starts a new row."

I thought it would be easy, and not even my fearing soul worried because my own grandfather held the whip. He carried it like it might bite *him.*

But soon I fell behind. I finished the first row last among everyone, so I lost my rest. I tried to go faster on the next row. I pushed my stick hard to make a hole and broke off the end, just the smallest bit of it. When Grandfather looked again, he saw the stick. He saw my seed mounds. "They're too close together, Bartolina! That part of the row will have to be done over."

I was already so far behind that Grandfather fixed the bad part of my row. As he finished, Don Luciano arrived on horseback. "Alfonso, a *mayordomo* gets work out of people. He doesn't do it for them."

I thought of Father as I worked the next row. How many times had I seen him on our plot? He never repeated a row because he always took the greatest care. More than once he said, "A seed treated badly doesn't give anything back." I tried to take care, but soon Grandfather came pleading. "You must go faster, Bartolina."

Don Luciano also returned. Grandfather didn't even wait for his complaint. "This girl's never planted before. She's the one who's been cleaning your house."

The administrator never looked at me. "Do you know how to crack that whip, Alfonso?"

Grandfather's obliging voice went shrill. "There's no need! I'll see that Bartolina learns. I'll see that she does the next row faster."

"Who said to strike the girl? I only want you to crack the whip. . . . Go on. Let me see you do it."

Grandfather swung the whip. It flopped over like a worm with fever.

"No, no. Get it into the air, like you're tossing it behind you. Then thrust forward, hard!" He made Grandfather try and try—until my fearing soul wanted to scream with each crack. Never did I work so hard as on that day.

I thought the broad bean planting would never end. Even when it did, there was still oca planting and then the potato planting. Nothing went well. Don Luciano became more and more cross as he saw how little we could plant. Only half the usual land was planted for the *patrón* that season. It was the same on our plot and on plots all over Masuru.

Then, five nights before All Souls' Day, the lazy brothers Wind and Hail conspired more fiercely than they had for many years. Some bean plants and most of the tiny oca and potato sprouts broke under their angry beating.

While everyone else worried about the crop, Doña Hilde seemed always to be inkweaving. She would sit and sit at the eating table or in Don Luciano's *oficina*. When I could, I would look up, just for a moment, to watch her hand and inkstick dancing together.

"There's much more need for words-on-paper," Manuela said. "The señora is sending them to Don Luciano's sons in the Chaco—they've joined the war now. Her Oruro people also sent officers to the Chaco, so she's keeping up with news to them, too."

With the planting finished, I again worked at the house three days each week. Well into the green season, the señora began handing me little paper pouches. These held the inkweavings closed inside, and I was to take them to Cauquimarca for her.

"What if I can't find a traveler going to Oruro?" I asked the first time. "What if I can't find one going to Don Luciano's sons in the Chaco?"

"Bartolina, what are you talking about? You take them to the store in Cauquimarca and leave them for the next post driver. I'll give you centavos to pay the postage." That confused me, and Doña Hilde shook her head crossly. "Must everything be explained?"

"Why not just give a potato?" She showed me her hardest eyes, and I quickly learned about the circles of metal called centavos. Soon I recognized the sun, the mountain, and the llama—an image that gave centavos their power.

Sometimes the post would bring inkweavings for Doña Hilde, and I would carry them back. Once when I gave her some, she turned to the administrator, who was taking coca tea at the eating table. "Luciano, there is news from each of your sons."

His glad smile started me thinking and thinking. Ink-weavings could carry words to the Chaco, and they could carry words back. I had never before asked anything from Doña Hilde, but that day I went pleading. "Señora, I have not seen my father in more than a year. He went among the first twenty men called. I need his news. Will you help me ask for it with words-on-paper?"

She sighed. "You'd have to know where he is."

"In the Chaco! He went to chase the Guaraní."

"Well, the Chaco is a huge place. Thousands of men are there. You would have to tell me the numbers of his division and troop. You would need to tell me his captain's name."

"Señora, I don't know those things."

"Well then, nothing can be done." She turned away, and I went home crying.

But on the next market day, I saw Guillermo Quispe drinking with two old men in Cauquimarca. "I have pay from the war," he told them. "I'm going to sponsor the Easter feast. Maybe I'll hire a brass band, like the one I saw in Sucre on the way to the Chaco."

A brass band? Still, I had other questions. Guillermo listened. Then he told me numbers for the division and troop that he and Father had served. I repeated and repeated them so that I'd be certain to remember them for the señora. Then Guillermo told me the name of the captain. "Maybe he'll help your father send news. If not, there's a man, Diego, who knows words-on-paper. He'll surely help Donato."

I didn't wait for my next day working in the hacienda house. I rushed straight to Doña Hilde.

"Your father would never answer you, Bartolina."

"Señora?"

"If he received your words, would he know what they were?"

"His captain will repeat them from the paper."

"Bartolina, captains in the Chaco have their hands full without doing chores for *indios*." She made the last word sound like *thief*.

"There is a man Diego. Guillermo Quispe said he would help."

"Bartolina, Guillermo drinks quantities of *chicha*. You cannot go by what he says."

That time I left angry—angry like Grandmother—but my fearing soul kept my confronting soul quiet. I longed for my cousin Dionisio. He might know enough about the ink-weaving. That reminded me of the one other person who might be able to help.

For the next month I thought and thought about the Baptist. I listened for people wailing about eaten children, but none ever did. No one repeated Fortunato's warning.

Still, I worried. With men and men dying in the Chaco, why bother with sorry accounts of a few children? And a wicked condor would be careful. The Baptist would know about brothers and sisters and cousins spreading tales. So he'd look for children without many people close by, maybe those with fathers off in the Chaco.

Could a pact be made with him? Maybe, but I couldn't take him a lamb. What would we eat? How would we weave? That made me think of my shawl, the one with the train of llamas woven through it. I didn't want to give my best shawl, but I *had* to know about Father.

I decided to take the risk. I wrapped my shawl around my shoulders the next time Doña Hilde sent me to Cauquimarca. Leaving the post, I walked beyond the square for the first time ever. I only stopped when I stood facing the Baptist's truck. Its two glass eyes held me frozen a few steps away from the Baptist's door. I never called out. I just stood there, frightened.

"Do you look for me, girl?"

The Baptist had appeared behind me. Maybe he'd come from visiting a house across the road. Then I saw blue sky in his strangest of eyes. Maybe he'd flown down behind me.

"Do you want to speak with me, girl?"

I thought of Father. I pushed back my fearing soul. "Grandfather," I said to the Baptist, "I need to know about Father."

"Your father? Who's that? Tell me his name."

I opened my mouth but then waited while my fearing soul whispered a warning. Maybe the Baptist wanted power over Father. "He went with the first men."

The Baptist took a step closer to me. "What first men?"

I stood caught between him and his truck. I spun, looking at the huge, round truck eyes. They just stared. I turned back toward the flaming red hair. "The men from a year ago." I held out a corner of my shawl. "Grandfather, can you . . . ?"

"Calm yourself, child."

Always he made the Aymara words sound so strange.

"Come, sit with me on my step."

The step right by the truck's eyes!

"You can call me Brother."

I gasped. A trick to anger Casimiro? My *angelito* might return and hear his own sister calling Brother to someone else.

I broke running to one side. I crossed the road and veered back toward the square. Rushing as quickly as I could, I looked for the shadow of wings overtaking me.

"Wait, girl! Don't be afraid." The Baptist used a high, obliging voice, like Grandfather's. I was sure that a condor would never use such a voice—except as a trick.

March 1934–January 1935

I sat eating bird stew with my grandparents when I thought about Guillermo's brass band. I didn't know what to imagine, so I asked.

Grandmother was surprised. "Guillermo is sponsoring the Easter feast? Bartolina, expect nothing until you see it."

Grandfather explained: "Think what Guillermo must be feeling, seeing women in the fields while he can't work. Whatever he manages, Bartolina, we must tell him it's the best feast ever."

Don Luciano first had tried Guillermo as a *mayordomo,* but his walking stick found soft spots in the soil and sank. Guillermo would get mad when he couldn't manage and madder yet if anyone tried to help. So the administrator told him to tend mules. Then Guillermo kept spilling feed sacks. Soon Don Luciano expected nothing.

The only thing Guillermo did was hobble to Cauqui-marca and put down his war centavos for *chicha.* Then, four days before Easter, Grandmother saw him begging from market women.

The next day, I began resewing loose matting in the ha-cienda house. Don Luciano appeared in a rage. He yelled for his youngest son. When Rómulo came, the administra-tor held out a pistol—not to shoot, just to show. Still, I was frightened because I could smell its smoke. Don Luciano pointed toward his *oficina*. "In there!" he ordered Rómulo.

I didn't hear everything through the door, only the administrator's loudest shouts. "Weapons are kept locked— always! . . . He was a Chaco veteran; certainly he knew guns! . . . 'Little harm done' is not the issue! What if he had stolen it with other intentions?"

Before dark, all Masuru knew that Guillermo Quispe had killed himself with Rómulo's pistol. But soon they began saying that he'd fallen in the Chaco. This was a kindness to his people, but it was also true. The war sometimes did its killing far beyond Boquerón and Nanawa.

Could it kill a hacienda?

I think yes because in the next year it almost killed Masuru. Don Luciano went wild over the poor harvest. More than once I heard him shouting at the *mayordomos:* "Not one potato, not one bean can be missed! How can I show the *patrón* a harvest like this?"

Our plots gave just as poorly. "I can't remember a harvest this bad," Grandmother told Grandfather when she counted our potatoes and ocas. "You must tell Don Luciano that some of the *patrón*'s crops must be given to each Masuru family."

"Will the *patrón* be generous when he has so little of his own for the markets?" Grandfather asked. His eyes seemed not to see. Just hearing his voice, I knew that no food would be given to us.

During the harvest, that boy Raúl lost one of our lambs to foxes. Grandmother was mad, but not with Raúl. Everyone had wanted his help. He had to watch a hundred sheep spread wide across the thin grass. It was easy for the foxes.

My grandparents began eating less, saving what they could. I said I didn't want much, but Grandmother scolded. "You need your strength, Bartolina."

She was right. I thought the next planting would be easier. Masuru had strong young men, those who had been boys the year before. But as the ground was being prepared, Salamanca's trucks came again. They took all those young men. They took other men who had been too old the year before. How can a man be too old for the Chaco one year but young enough the next? Still, the trucks took them.

Silently, secretly, my confronting soul sent the Virgin of Copacabana my angriest prayer. It asked her to turn Salamanca to stone.

In the fields, I poked holes, dropped seeds, covered, and measured. Sometimes I left just one soul repeating and repeating the tasks. The others would go looking—for Father; for Uncle, Aunt, and my cousins; for Simona.

When the planting finally ended, the news from the Chaco seemed to come all at once. The market women began to say that the entire Chaco would be lost. "The Guaraní have pushed us out of our own oil lands near Tarija," said one.

We heard talk of a great new battle at El Carmen, but no one could say things about Father or any other Masuru man. I wondered if they were being killed as I carried spices from Cauquimarca or made wood shine in the hacienda house.

People began saying that the Guaraní might *overrun* Tarija. Why worry about some faraway place that I had never heard of before that season? But then a market woman said, "Bolivia will defend her cities to the last man." I cried. Father was one of those men—if he still lived.

I never expected the kind Virgin to answer my angry prayer, but soon, all the market women were talking about Salamanca. "After El Carmen, he went to scold his generals. They turned on him! The *presidente* is under arrest."

That was the last news I ever heard about Salamanca, but news of his war still came and came. The whole time, we tried to live through the hardest growing season ever. Families had always taken sheep for meat, but never so many.

My grandparents and I had two sheep left. One we killed two weeks after All Souls' Day, and Grandmother cut two tiny pieces of meat. She burned one in the far pastures and appealed to the grandfather of Illampu to share small game. She left the other at Cauquimarca's shrine to the Virgin of Copacabana. She prayed not for plenty, but for just enough to keep us alive. At market she traded a little meat for salt to keep the rest from spoiling.

Grandfather began hunting on every night that had a bright moon. He weighted a basket with stones, propped it on a stick, and left a tiny bit of meat underneath. From hiding, he pulled a length of yarn to make the basket fall over any bird or viscacha that came for the meat. But poor Grandfather! He was thin and weak by then. Most nights he came home shivering with nothing in his basket.

One family in the north part of Masuru killed a young llama for food! I'd never heard of such a thing. Sheep almost disappeared at Masuru. All weaving stopped. Of all my souls, my weaving soul was the most troubled.

Once, just before dawn, Grandfather caught a viscacha, but it bit him as he killed it. He was still bleeding when he got it home. Grandmother told him to stay and sleep. "Be wise like the llama, who refuses too great a load."

Grandfather thought only of his buckets. "I have my obligations, Julia. Tonight we'll eat well. Then I'll rest."

That morning, he brought only one load of water. Much later, when he hadn't returned, Manuela sent me looking. I found him lying halfway between the stream and the hacienda house, not one single drop spilled from the buckets beside him.

I held his head in my lap. He tried to speak, but no words came. I begged him to be still; then I ran shouting and shouting until I was sure that others had heard. Weeping, I hurried back to Grandfather and tried to give him water, just the smallest bit from my hand. It only spilled down his cheek.

Don Luciano knelt beside us. He felt Grandfather's face. Then he called to the Virgin and made the sign of the cross. Manuela came next and began the wailing for the dead.

Because Grandfather had died with his eyes open, Grandmother said he was looking for souls to steal. To prevent this, she put a cord of woven palm leaves around his neck and pulled it tight.

Masuru people came visiting our house while he lay there waiting to go to the cemetery. They turned their clothes wrong side out to honor him. We did the same and gave up all spices for a month.

Don Luciano didn't turn his clothes, but he honored Grandfather with words: "What a fine example for every Masuru tenant!"

Doña Hilde, standing at his side, wouldn't turn her clothes either. She wouldn't even look at Grandfather, and I wondered if she feared losing a soul. Did she think the cord was loose? The señora almost seemed sick.

Don Luciano saw to Grandfather's burial. He had two boys dig a grave in the Ch'oke part of the cemetery. Since Padre Roberto was not expected that season, the administrator repeated his words for all the Masuru people who went there: "Alfonso Ch'oke led an exemplary life."

Again I watched Doña Hilde. Something seemed wrong. With Don Luciano showing kindness to Grandfather, I decided to show kindness to his wife.

"Señora," I asked, "do you want to jump over the grave

~ 74 ~

before we close it?" I used the Spanish words, saying them just right, yet she didn't understand.

I pointed. "Look." A mother led a sick boy to the grave. He jumped over. An old woman with fever jumped, too, and people on each side helped so that she didn't fall. "Grandfather's departing souls will carry away whatever troubles you, Señora."

She gave me hard eyes. She never answered me. As more people came to jump, she whispered to Don Luciano—I just barely heard. "Are you going to let this continue?"

Her question scared me. I was relieved only when the administrator answered. "Hilde, I wouldn't think of stopping it. I have to keep the peace around here."

April 1935, Maya

A new harvest ended Masuru's worst starving season. Of those people who had counted themselves as Masuru's oldest when the green season began, most lay in the cemetery. A few had faced the lazy brothers in the hills instead of taking food from their people.

When Grandmother saw that Pachamama was again sending only the poorest of crops, she let me hear her hardest questions. With no new wool, how could we keep warm when our clothes grew ragged? How could we eat during the ice time and still have seed potatoes at the next planting?

Then she began telling and telling things. She spoke about men and women and babies, all the things that Mother would have told me. I was nearly thirteen, old enough to hear, but Grandmother had still another reason for explaining. I remembered how Basilia had explained things—just before her time to leave the pasture.

A week before Easter, Grandmother and I gathered a few small potatoes from our plot. "This time, you'll make the *chuño*," she told me. "We'll see how you do on your own." She watched me crush the potatoes and prepare the mash. She asked which hilltop I'd choose to be certain that the lazy brother Frost found the batch (for in *chuño*-making, we always tricked him into helping us). She asked how I'd protect it from animals while the nights and days of freezing and thawing turned it into *chuño*.

For the first time, she said what I knew she'd been thinking. "You need to be sure of these things, Bartolina, because maybe soon I'll be lying beside my Juan."

I'd heard Juan Caranavi's name whispered and whispered that season. A soul of longing always stood behind the whispers. Questions and questions came into my mind. Why did Grandfather Juan lie buried among thieves when he was no thief? Why did Masuru people come sneaking with woven flowers to honor him? I had always worried that Grandmother would be mad at me for wondering about things that weren't my business. I still worried, but I asked just the same. "What happened in Grandfather's uprising?"

Grandmother found me with curious eyes, so I explained what I'd heard at Carnival—a Carnival with little music and no feasting. "That old curer Arturo sat whispering. He spoke of a day when Grandfather Juan's confronting soul chased off the *patrón*. The other old men shushed him right away, but first I heard him say 'the uprising.'"

Grandmother gazed toward Illampu for the longest time. All at once she began speaking and speaking.

"When I was small, the southern part of Masuru was Aymara land. The families all together held it as one land, and each year they decided which family would plant each plot. Then the *wirajjocha* said that our way was no good. They said one part of the land belonged to the Ch'okes, another part to the Chinapiris, and on and on. They said it was the law. Land had to be held that way."

"But the land was ours?"

Grandmother nodded. "The father of our *patrón* held some of the land, too, the part with the hacienda house and on north. He came sneaking down, first to one family, then

~ 77 ~

to the next. I remember when he came to our house. He showed my father more silver than he'd ever seen in his life. 'See,' he told Father. 'Your land isn't worth half this much silver, but I want more land near what I already have. That's why I'll do you the favor of giving so much.'

"It was the same with other families. The old *patrón* let each man hold the silver in his hands. Ch'okes, Cácereses, Quispes, Chinapiris—he tricked them all."

Grandmother seemed small and tired. "Those men didn't know what land came to in silver."

"Caranavis were tricked, too?"

"Juan's father was deceived like the rest. Juan was with him when he went asking to buy new land north of Macata. The *patrón* there just laughed in their faces. He said they'd need twenty times the silver just to get back the amount of land they'd given up.

"They came back to Masuru, begging to use their old land. They had to promise service to the *patrón*. And service and *service*."

After these angry words, she calmed herself before saying more. "Fifteen ice seasons and green seasons passed. That old *patrón* died, and his son took the land. Then, in the year that your mother was waiting to be born, Wind and Hail came viciously—twice.

"The food from the plots and the *patrón*'s wide fields— all of it taken together—was only just enough to keep the Masuru people alive. But our *patrón* was young and foolish and greedy. He'd given only promises in exchange for that Yungas plantation, and he needed silver to make the promises good. He told us that nothing had changed. He called for mules and llamas to take his crops away to market.

"That year a puma came out of the mountains, the last one ever to stalk Masuru sheep. Juan killed it with sling and spear. People looked to him. He was respected! He drank that puma's blood for courage and made a war speech against the *patrón*. Everyone heard. Even two *mayordomos* listened and stood with Juan."

"The *patrón* fled?"

Grandmother nodded. "Your grandfather took back Masuru for us—for eleven days." She went silent.

"And then?" I asked.

"Soldiers, Bartolina. A *patrón* can summon soldiers. A hundred came, every one with a rifle. What could we do?"

Grandmother told me every last thing. Nineteen Masuru men were leaned against the wall of the hacienda house and whipped. The two *mayordomos*, whose people had lived at Masuru since far-past times, were chased off the land. One man, my grandfather, Juan Caranavi, was shot.

Maybe it was wrong to ask Grandmother about the uprising. That same hour, in my anger against the *wirajjocha*, I repeated Doña Hilde's words about the grave jumping. I *know* that was wrong. I never saw Grandmother's eyes so fierce!

Concevida stopped me on the road the next day. "Bartolina, you have to calm your grandmother. She's going from house to house whispering." Concevida whispered herself. "She wants an uprising. She wants to seize the *patrón*'s crops."

My eyes went wide. "A *patrón* can summon soldiers!"

"So I told her. She just says that our men are the soldiers now. But, Bartolina, the *patrón* wouldn't call *them*. They'd call soldiers from others places."

I decided to confront Grandmother, but my fearing soul didn't want to face her hardest eyes. Each day, I decided to confront her on the next.

Then came Easter, and there *was* a feast. It was the smallest, but we did eat and listen to the pipes and drums.

Grandmother seemed completely calm, and I thought the music had settled her. I decided I wouldn't have to speak against her uprising at all.

Two days later, I went to Cauquimarca to see if there were inkweavings for Doña Hilde. Felicia, the woman at the store, told me that a post driver would be there soon.

Having to wait, I asked, "What news does the war send?"

Felicia always heard a lot. "The Guaraní thought they could take Tarija and our oil fields. Ha! They've come so far across the Chaco that it's difficult for their people to supply them."

"What does it mean?"

"Well, the Guaraní are like anyone else. To shoot, they need bullets. And the colder days are coming. They need clothes and blankets. They aren't getting them."

"Maybe our men will come back soon."

Felicia shrugged. "Maybe. They say our men are fighting back hard. We've had a big victory at Villa Montes."

It had been seasons and seasons since I'd been so hopeful. When the post driver brought a letter for Doña Hilde, I went smiling toward the hacienda house.

Even before I reached it, all my happiness fled.

April 1935, Paya

In the distance I saw Grandmother coming along the road. An old *mayordomo* followed a few steps behind. He was speaking, but she never once turned toward him. The whole time her eyes held the administrator's gate.

She never touched the latch. She seized the gate and shook it and shook it.

"Don Luciano!" Grandmother demanded.

Coming nearer, I heard Manuela. "Julia, do you want trouble for all of us? He's taking tea with the señora."

"Don Luciano!" Grandmother shouted.

"It's all right, Manuela." The administrator appeared at the carved doors. His voice sent no anger, no fear, no excitement—just words. "Unlatch the gate before Julia Caranavi breaks it down."

The gate opened, but Grandmother didn't enter. I stopped beside the *mayordomo,* who'd stayed a few steps behind her. I could see only her black braids hanging behind, but Manuela could see her eyes. I never saw the cook looking so frightened.

By spreading his hands, the administrator asked Grandmother why his tea had been disturbed.

"Why does your *mayordomo* say that I must go to the Yungas?"

The *mayordomo* spoke firmly. "Don Luciano does not have to explain his—"

"Why does this fool say that I must go to the Yungas?"

Manuela's mouth fell open. Don Luciano only crossed his arms. "Where are the woven goods you owe to the *patrón*?"

"Can I weave water from the streams? There are no sheep. There's no wool."

"I could send you off to fend for yourself, but I can see that these are hard times. That's why I've done you the favor of finding useful work for you. You'll go to the *patrón*'s plantation house in the Yungas."

"I live here."

"The war has disrupted things at the plantation house, too. The cook is a young woman, very able to work in the orchards. You'll take over her job in the kitchen."

"I will not go."

Don Luciano shrugged. "You are a free woman, but not free to trespass. Accept the work I offer you or take the road out of Masuru."

"I live in Donato Ch'oke's house, and he is serving this very moment. He fights in the Chaco. Do you forget?"

"I haven't forgotten Donato's service. That's exactly why I am being so reasonable." The administrator also had strong eyes. Seeing them, I understood something. The whispering had reached him. He knew of Grandmother's talk of an uprising.

"Masuru people respect the woman of Juan Caranavi," she said. "What will they do if I'm sent away?"

The administrator shrugged. "I'm kindly giving you a chance to make a living, Julia. Why should that upset one single person?"

"Tell the *patrón* to give me a ewe and a ram," Grandmother said. "Soon there will be weaving for him again."

Don Luciano seemed not to hear. "A mule train will be

resting here tomorrow, Julia. When it starts toward the Yungas the day after, you'll be going with it."

Bent over wide fields the next day, I helped with the *patrón*'s oca harvest. I kept straightening, watching for the mules and hoping that they'd lose their way. But when the sun was highest, I saw two market men leading them down the road from Cauquimarca.

An hour after they stopped at Masuru's stables, Grandmother came along the same road—from the cemetery. Then she walked toward us, the first time I'd ever seen her in the *patrón*'s fields. Thirty Masuru people stopped their work and went silent when she raised a long spear.

"Juan Caranavi calls for war!" she shouted. "When the sun is low, Masuru people will meet at the stable. We will seize a mule and offer its blood to Pachamama."

Weary mothers watched with frightened eyes. Thin children peered from behind their skirts. Old men slowly straightened their backs, then looked among themselves, one to the next. The oldest, Justo Carrillo, stepped toward Grandmother.

"Julia, look around," he said with a voice deep and soft. "The time isn't right. We'll stand with you—but not in war. We'll tell Don Luciano that you're too old to travel. If all of us speak together, he'll listen."

She seemed not to hear. "From the moment that Pachamama receives our offering, the food she sends will stay here. The market beasts will carry away no beans, no ocas, no white potatoes, no bitter potatoes—not even one. Masuru people will eat the harvest of *our* lands."

"Look at your spearhead, Julia," Justo said. We could all see its dull, round tip. "That's a dancer's spear. It's no good for war."

"The beasts will carry fleeing *wirajjocha*, nothing else."

"A *patrón* can summon soldiers," shouted one of the mothers.

Grandmother laughed. "The soldiers will stand with us. Our own Masuru men are the soldiers now."

"Julia," said Justo. "There are soldiers and soldiers from all across Kollasuyo. The *wirajjocha* won't choose Masuru men to send against us."

"Juan has spoken!"

Grandmother turned and began walking toward a field where other Masuru people were gathering broad beans.

Much later, I followed Justo when he went to the hacienda house to speak against sending Grandmother away. But Manuela said that Don Luciano wasn't there. Justo went looking to the north.

I went the other way, past the stable. Four men stood guard there—Rómulo, a *mayordomo,* and the two who were traveling with the mule train. I knew then that Grandmother's war speech had been repeated to the administrator.

Soon I found Don Luciano. He and another *mayordomo* were searching through every house and cookhouse in the south of Masuru. But they couldn't find Grandmother.

I stood trying to decide what to do when the softest whisper sneaked from behind me. "Julia's in the hills somewhere." It was the widow Concevida. "I saw her going east, carrying a blanket and spear."

I thought of Grandmother under the wide sky. I couldn't see a single cloud, and I feared that the lazy brother Frost would come fiercely in the darkness. Already the sun stood close to the lake.

Concevida saw me looking. "We can't possibly go searching this late. Come to my house as soon as there's light tomorrow. Then we'll search."

I said I would and started home, but I kept thinking. What if I didn't wait for old, slow Concevida? What if I ran all the way? Maybe I could bring Grandmother back to the house under the first stars—before the lazy brother came. I had to try. I hadn't calmed her war talk, so it was my doing that left her under the sky.

I passed Chuyma running. The sun had already reached its red time. Soon after, while I spied from a high hill close to the mountains, it slipped away.

"Grandmother!" I called and called. My breathing was quick and my voice was small among the hills and hills. I began to worry about *myself* under the wide sky. I knew the foxes ran at night.

And what of the Baptist? Maybe he'd been watching ever since I showed myself to him. Maybe he'd strike the moment he saw me shivering and weak.

I prayed to the grandfather of Illampu, and he helped. The white cap of his great mountain held the sun just a little longer, and its light let me find my way.

I began to run surely because one of my souls remembered something. Hadn't Grandmother once told Father to hide from Salamanca's trucks? Hadn't she said a cave lay under Iquiña?

I approached the evil hill, thinking the whole time about souls of unbaptized babies that might be wandering there. I thought about the bad luck that might be swirling around Casimiro's twin, my unnamed sister. I had no coca shreds to drop as tribute, so I pulled out one eyebrow hair and left her that.

Just a moment later, I saw a boulder below Iquiña. It was catching the smallest bit of a glow from somewhere. I pulled my shawl tight around my shoulders and hurried toward the light.

Among huge boulders, Grandmother sat by a tiny *yareta* fire, leaning close over the shaft of the dancer's spear. Her eyes showed surprise at my movement, but only for a moment. When she saw it was me, that I'd come alone, she turned back to her work. She wound yarn tightly around the shaft to hold a new head fast.

"Grandmother, we have to go back." I could already see the first stars.

"We stay among the hills tonight."

"Grandmother, this is Iquiña. We can't stay beside the evil hill all night."

"Calm yourself. Tomorrow, go to the hacienda house and—"

"I *will* go. I'll tell Don Luciano you're too old to travel to the Yungas. Justo Carrillo will stand with me."

"Bartolina, listen! Take a flat stone to the hacienda house. Then find a glass drinking jar in Manuela's cooking place. Smash it. Crush it under the stone. Then, when Manuela is making bread, tell her Doña Hilde is calling. With Manuela gone, sprinkle the glass into the dough. Be careful! The glass will be sharp."

I gasped. I knew in an instant that I never could follow her plan, not even against Don Luciano. "Grandmother, what if *Manuela* eats some of the—"

"Hush! Later, when Don Luciano lies weak and bleeding, I will come. I will bring spears and throwing slings for all brave Masuru people. No *wirajjocha* will molest us after that."

"Grandmother, what if I can't do it?"

"You can! And when Masuru people see that one girl has beaten the administrator, they'll find the courage to stand against the *patrón*."

"But the soldiers! A *patrón* can summon soldiers."

"Stop your trembling! Do you want to chase dust forever?" Grandmother shook with anger. "Do you want your fingers to grow old and stiff weaving for the *patrón*?"

Then she calmed herself and held the spearhead toward

me. "Whose grandchild are you? Touch the point for courage."

I obeyed, but carefully. That point was a stone thorn. Had she made it? So quickly? I drew my hand back without finding any courage. My fearing soul sent sobbing and more tears.

"Bartolina! Stop your crying." She pointed. "Go inside."

I wanted to obey, yet what did she mean? "Grand-mother?"

She led me to a small opening that hid itself among the boulders—the cave. "There's a blanket inside. We'll wrap ourselves against the cold and speak more about courage."

The morning glow found the cave mouth. I awoke, maybe to the sound of a voice. I listened.

"Don Rómulo!" That time I was sure. It was a *mayordomo* calling out.

"Grandmother," I whispered.

She wasn't there. Maybe she'd gone out spying or collecting *yareta*. I crawled toward the daylight. I had to stop and close my eyes against the brightness. Half of me crouched under the sky, the rest in the cave's darkness.

Soon I could see the *mayordomo* at the foot of Iquiña, not far away, and I kept still. As Rómulo walked closer, the *mayordomo* pointed toward boulders just up the slope. "Old Julia is hiding right up there." He began climbing the hill.

Rómulo took his pistol from its pouch and pointed toward the sky. Maybe he meant to call his father with a shot. Instead, he went stiff.

I followed his wide eyes just quickly enough to see Grandmother jabbing her spear at the *mayordomo*. He leaned wildly to save his face, and his foot lost the slope. He fell hard and lay gasping. Grandmother rushed past him toward Rómulo.

The mountain cats of far-past days were gone before my time at Masuru, but it wasn't so with Grandmother. As she aimed her spear in the last instant of her war, all her souls together found a voice I'd never heard.

It must have been the scream of a puma.

April 1935, Quimsa

Maybe the grandfather of Lake Titicaca gives a *totora* reed for every potato sent by Pachamama. I saw uncountable thousands along his shore. On the waters beyond, two fishermen, each in his own boat, dragged a net between them. But who could call out over such a distance? I didn't try.

Around me stood Huarina's market square, but it wasn't a market day. I saw no one. I don't know how long I stood. Maybe for a heartbeat. Maybe for an hour. Finally a market man came from a stable with a feed sack for his mule.

I went to him. "Father, is Simona Páez nearby?"

At first he just stared back. Even the mule seemed nervous with me there. I was weary from walking and stumbling. Dust and dust covered the llamas on my shawl. My skirt was soiled and torn. My hands were dirty and sore. The woven strap of one sandal was broken. Its loose strands hung long enough to tie easily. Any weaver could have done it. How I'd tried!

Finally, "Girl, what's happened to you?"

I went stiff. Maybe he'd heard of Soledad Girón, the girl with the lost souls. Seeing *me*, what did he suspect?

"Girl, who are your people?"

"Father, please, just tell me where to find Simona Páez."

Soon I was walking again. Past the square, I saw two houses just off the road to Achacachi. Beyond them I went and went and went, looking for more houses. The market man had said to look for three together, well back from the road. I found them, all sitting close to the lake. I needed no more questions. Simona came walking toward me even before I reached her house.

I saw her anger the moment she recognized me. She stopped ten steps away. All the time walking, I'd been afraid that she would still hate me.

Then she took in everything the market man had seen. Her anger changed to a frightened wondering.

"Bartolina, are your people near?" This was Juana. She'd come looking behind her daughter.

I didn't know what to answer. I only stared at the soil.

"Your father didn't come back from the Chaco?"

Except for the wounded, what man had? I shook my head.

"Where's your grandfather?"

"Lying in the cemetery since before the harvest."

"Your grandmother?"

I gasped. I opened my mouth, but no words came.

"Bartolina, where's your grandmother?" These were the first words Simona had spoken to me.

"Shhh! Don't you see she's had a fright?" Juana took my arm. "You'll sleep in my uncle's house tonight."

Simona took my other arm. Later, in front of a house made all of reeds, she tied my sandal strap—easily. I thanked her, but only through my own weeping.

The reed house belonged to Juana's Uncle Tulio, a man who knew the lake the way Father knew the soil. When I first saw him, he was carrying a huge net folded over his shoulder. Whenever he gathered fish or *totora* reeds, he threw coca and hot spices into the water—tribute for the lake's grandfather.

Juana and Simona didn't always live with him. They had people all across Kollasuyo. Sometimes they lived with Juana's brother in Achacachi, and once a year they went to a cousin in La Paz.

"Each way we carry things," Simona explained as she helped Tulio make a new boat. It was twice as long as a man, with ends that stood high, like proud llama heads. "We take potatoes or mats down to La Paz. We bring back fine belts and tin pots. When we're in the country, we help with planting and harvests—and boats. In the town, we help with small children or with the marketing if someone is sick."

I was glad that Simona wanted to tell me things. Yet, we didn't talk like best friends. She'd gone back to pulling at her braids and seemed always to look down or to one side.

She and her mother wanted to do whatever they could for the people who took them in. I could see why. With Tulio were a son, the son's wife, and five little ones. The house had two rooms, but both small. Things were hard when Juana and Simona came. They were harder still when I came.

Simona thought of something. "Remember that Basilia who used to be at Masuru? Isn't she one of your people?"

"She is, but I don't know how to find her—or any of my family."

"I saw a woman selling fruit in La Paz last year. I think it was her."

Tulio never looked away from his boat. "Simona, hold the end of this reed." Then he said, "Bartolina can stay in my house until you go to La Paz. Then you can take her looking for that Basilia." I felt my first happiness since coming to Huarina. Still, I wondered if Simona wanted me back with my people just to have me away from her.

A few days later, she came listening quietly when her mother and I sat outside the house. Juana spoke: "Bartolina, you should tell someone—maybe old Concevida—that you're going to La Paz. If not, what will your father think when he comes back from the Chaco?"

I didn't want to risk facing a *mayordomo* who knew I had run away from my service, who knew whose granddaughter I was. I dreaded walking again where that Baptist might strike from sky or ground.

"I think maybe Father fell in the Chaco," I said. One of my souls raged against these words, and right away I saw the pain in Juana's eyes. But I would have spoken anything to keep from returning to Masuru. I began to weep. Mostly I feared a fierce confronting soul, newly loose to sweep across the hacienda like a raging puma.

"Don't say he fell!" Juana calmed me with talk about Father, saying things I'd never known. "When we first went to Masuru, we were sent to one of the poorest plots. Some said that it hadn't lain fallow long enough, but Donato told Evaristo ways to make things grow. He gave him the shoulder blade of a llama and showed him the easiest way to turn the soil with it. Donato's a good man, Bartolina, so close to Pachamama. He needs to be able to find you."

"I . . . can't go back to Masuru." Slowly I told about the war speech and the night at Iquiña. Through tears, I even spoke about the terrible morning and Grandmother's war cry.

"Rómulo shot her?"

I nodded. "She fell backward and never moved again."

"What a fright." Juana held my shoulders. "But that day is finished. Calm yourself. It won't come again."

I wouldn't calm myself. "I was stupid! I shrieked as Grandmother fell. Before then, no one had seen me."

"Bartolina, why worry?"

I moaned. "I was still half in the cave. Rómulo came looking and found the entrance. He pulled out weapons and weapons. He worried and worried when he saw the sharpened spearheads, a hundred of them. He only calmed himself when Don Luciano showed him that the sling cords and spear shafts were rotten. D'you see? They were from a far-past uprising. That place under Iquiña was my Grandfather Juan's war cave."

"You're afraid that Don Luciano will blame you for the Caranavi war calls?"

I wasn't especially afraid of that. The administrator never spoke a single fierce word to me in the whole time it took to carry Grandmother back across the pastures. I was more worried that he might someday tell me to weave for the *patrón.*

Still, I nodded to Juana. I didn't tell her everything.

June 1935, Maya

Juana went alone to Masuru and gave my news to
Concevida. A few days later, we started toward La
Paz. Juana and Simona wore the bright shawls of market
women. They set their little bowlers just so on their heads.
Their town shoes hid their toes. I had only open sandals
and my frayed Masuru clothes and shawl. We walked, leading Tulio's mule, loaded high with reed mats for the town
markets.

Tulio took us safely along the road. He brought an ar-
madillo shell with three cords pulled tightly over it. The
whole time we traveled, he coaxed music from it—not feast
songs, just the *brrii brrii brrii* of a walking strum.

We followed the line of peaks southward. "Do you see
that huge mountain with three peaks?" Tulio asked.

"Illimani," I said. I knew the name of the most distant
mountain I had seen looking south from Masuru.

"Go toward it, and you'll find La Paz, the greatest town
in all Kollasuyo."

Something puzzled me. "That mountain isn't so far away.
Why can't I see this greatest town?"

Simona looked at me, smiling. She seemed more my
friend just then. "You'll see it."

Halfway through our second day walking, I noticed the

road ahead sinking away. Suddenly we stood at the edge of a bowl cut into the very face of Kollasuyo. Wide? Even a condor could grow weary flying across. And deep? Only Illimani lying down could ever fill it.

Cauquimarca would have been lost down there. Suddenly Huarina seemed like nothing. I knew La Paz would be bigger, but I thought I'd see just a big square with buildings and buildings running like a long fence around it. I *did* see a big square, but it sat like a tiny island in a wide lake of buildings! La Paz covered all the floor of that great bowl. It even tried to climb up the sides.

Our road didn't want to be too steep. So, instead of dropping straight in, it circled partly around the bowl as it took us down and down. After twenty steps, I looked far to the north and barely saw the top of Illampu. Soon I looked again, but I'd sunk too low to see above the edge of the bowl to Masuru's great peak. Why should a town—or I— hide from the grandfather of Illampu?

Trucks and trucks passed us each moment, and my fearing soul worried. Sometimes we had to press against the bowl's wall to let one by. Those going up moved slowly, and we saw two that were angry with the climb. A man opened the mouth of one of them, and a white cloud leaped from inside. He tried to appease the truck by giving a huge can of water as tribute. I heard a great hissing, and finally it calmed.

Trucks going down crept even more slowly. They didn't dare lose the road. Simona pointed to one that had. I saw it lying on its crushed top far down the steep slope.

The first places we passed looked like our Masuru houses, except they had roofs of tin, not thatch. Farther down stood the bigger places, all with red roofs like the one over the hacienda house. As we got lower, the buildings seemed to spread apart, showing us people and people and people.

Most of them dressed like market men and women, not like Masuru people. But when I saw faces and heard words, I found that most La Paz people were Aymara.

Still, in all my life I had never seen as many *wirajjocha* as I could take in with any single glance. Sometimes bunches stood all together. Simona asked me how well I knew the Spanish words.

"I learned them in the hacienda house."

"That's good. With Spanish and Aymara words, you can talk to anyone in La Paz."

I was glad. "It's not so different than the rest of Kollasuyo."

"Don't say 'Kollasuyo,'" Simona warned me. "Say 'La Paz Department.' Those are the Spanish words for our part of Kollasuyo, but everyone here uses them."

We reached the house of Juana's cousin. I saw the worry in his face at seeing me. And why not? His house was small, and six already lived there.

Simona was sent walking with me through the markets— even though things needed doing. That told me how anxious everyone was to have me find my family. But in La Paz I couldn't just call Basilia's name and have any market man point the way.

We searched the markets for a day and another and another. Simona and I walked over streets and streets of dust and streets and streets of stone. We saw coca leaves being sold in bags so big that llamas would surely refuse the load. We saw blankets in stacks and blankets hanging full out. We saw cups and plates and bowls polished to shine bright in the sun. We saw clay jars and pots like Father used to make. I couldn't open my eyes without seeing quantities of things.

No market ever seemed to be the last one. Most days we walked once or twice along the street where Simona had seen Basilia trading fruit the year before. Once we spent a whole day there. I asked people, "Do you know Basilia Ch'oke?" A boy watching cars said he knew many Basilias, but he never asked family names. I asked about Dionisio and Adela, about Uncle Jacinto and Aunt Cristina. It was always the same.

I saw one woman selling stacks of something. A *wirajjocha* man put down centavos and took one. He opened it into what seemed to be the thinnest blanket—all covered with inkweaving. "Market papers," Simona explained.

"What do they tell?"

Simona shrugged. "Maybe *wirajjocha* things."

We asked the woman if she knew Ch'okes. She said yes. We went running and even found an Adela Ch'oke, but she was an old woman who knew nothing of my Ch'okes.

Once we came to a small plaza. Just behind it stood a row of doorways of wood and glass. My chin went up, and I saw windows over windows. That place wanted to be a mountain, and it almost was.

But I didn't watch the building. I watched the *wirajjocha,* all grown, but none very old. At first I thought they were making a chain for a feast dance. But it wasn't a feast day, and I'd never once heard a feast song chanted with such anger. All those *wirajjocha* together made the same Spanish words. I listened—and was never so surprised: "Stop the war. Stop the war. Justice for *indio* soldiers."

Simona pointed. Three *wirajjocha* soldiers were coming— also looking angry. My fearing soul didn't want anyone thinking that I was standing where I shouldn't. Maybe those soldiers would say that I'd been chanting, too. What then? I took Simona's arm, and we hurried away.

The faces of La Paz began to make me think of the tiny sand grains beneath the streams of Masuru. I could look closely at any one, but how could I look closely at them all?

"I wish I'd talked to your cousin when I saw her," Simona told me. It was our sixth day searching. "I could have found out where your people live."

I wasn't mad. I knew why she hadn't. My cousins could tell La Paz people that Simona was a twin. "You didn't know I'd be coming," I said. "Why worry? We'll find them." But even as I spoke, I began to fear that we never would.

A blanket hanging from a market stall left a shady spot, and we rested. "You should make a blanket like that," Simona said. "Only you could put a train of llamas across it, just like on your shawl."

I surprised her. Right there in the market I began to weep.

"Bartolina, what's wrong?"

"I can't weave. I can *never* weave."

She seized my hands and looked at them. "Why not?"

"Maybe my hands can weave, but . . ."

"Bartolina, what?"

I'd never told anyone. "My weaving soul!"

I could see that Simona didn't understand. "Remember what I said about the cave? I was too afraid to strike against Don Luciano. Grandmother knew it, and my crying disgusted her. She didn't want any grandchild of Juan Caranavi to weave for the *patrón*. Later she wanted revenge against me for letting Rómulo find Grandfather's war cave."

"But she'd already died."

"Died with her eyes wide open! They were open the whole time it took the *mayordomos* to carry her out of the hills. There was no palm rope to hold her back from stealing souls. When I couldn't even fix my sandal strap, I knew she'd had her revenge."

"Can it be so?" my best friend asked. "When you're calm, we'll try some weaving."

"No!" I barely whispered the next thing. "It would be for nothing. Grandmother stole away my weaving soul."

June 1935, Paya

The next day a bellowing truck passed Simona and me and stopped in front of a market stall. I'd already seen the woman there. She wasn't Aunt or Basilia or Adela.

Two market men stepped out. By the time they reached the truck pen, the woman was already looking at figs and peaches and bananas, basketfuls fresh from the Yungas. She chose, and one man lifted down the baskets she wanted.

The other had turned mostly away, but I saw a thin square of wood in his hand. On it lay an inkweaving, one single leaf alone. As each basket came down, he made stitches in the inkweaving.

I was surprised when the woman gave nothing in return, no goods, no centavos. The truck men just closed the pen and began walking toward the front. I thought they'd forgotten to take their due, and I looked at their faces to see if they seemed young and foolish.

I was up before my next heartbeat. I didn't like trucks, but I rushed toward that one, shouting the whole way. The man with the inkweaving was my cousin Dionisio.

That truck howled and swayed and trembled—with me inside. Whenever it slowed, it screamed and tried to make me fall. Without my cousin's arm to hold, my fearing soul would have sent *me* screaming.

On the other side of me, Dionisio's friend Tomás stamped at the truck with his foot and made it bellow. His arms were strong for a man so thin, and it's a good thing. He had to hold that truck's inside wheel, and it tried to twist free like a struggling ram. I pressed close to Dionisio while Tomás somehow made that truck obey his will.

Only when it stopped and we were ready to climb down did I think of something else. "Dionisio, that market woman tricked you!"

"What?"

"She took those baskets. What did she give you for them?"

Dionisio's eyes asked if a more stupid girl had ever come down the slopes into La Paz. He waved his inkweaving in my face. "I have her on the manifest."

He had to explain. That inkweaving—the manifest—had been made in the Yungas by Señor Emilio Catari, a wealthy market man who owned three trucks. Whenever a basket was lifted into a truck pen, he made ink stitches on the manifest. Then he gave it over to his truck men.

"When a La Paz woman takes a basket, I put down her name. D'you see? With the manifest, there's no doubt. Don Emilio knows who took the fruit, and no one can say I've remembered wrong."

"Still, Dionisio, she didn't give you your due."

"How could she? She hasn't sold the fruit yet. When she does, she gives some of the centavos to us and keeps some for herself. Mother and Basilia and Adela all get centavos by selling Don Emilio's goods in the markets. Then Tomás and I get our due for helping with the truck and the manifest. The rest goes to Don Emilio."

"Why did the señor choose you?"

Tomás laughed and answered for my cousin. "Don Emilio sent me rushing to find Dionisio the moment he heard about him. How many boys coming into La Paz can see the words on a manifest?"

When I walked into Uncle's house, Basilia and Adela shouted my name, both in the same instant. Aunt wept.

Dionisio just worried about a girl with country looks standing beside him. "Can't we put her in decent clothes so people don't stare?" He used Spanish words to say this, never remembering that I'd worked in the hacienda house.

"Won't you take me to market for some, Cousin?" Then everyone stared at *him* because my Spanish words were as good as his. We all laughed hard, even Dionisio.

There was sadness, too. I told my cousins about our grandfather. They told me that Uncle had been called to the Chaco War six months earlier.

"He went just after the defeat at El Carmen," Dionisio said. "But he's showing those Guaraní now. All you hear about these days is the counteroffensive."

Aunt's eyes told me that she was not feeling quite so brave as her son. "Bartolina," she said before more war words could be spoken, "you know that this house is your house now."

I liked that house. Its roof was a sloped sheet of tin, strong enough that the lazy brother Hail could bang with rage and never worry anyone beneath. We could all sleep in either of two big rooms, and Aunt had a small cooking room, too. Behind was the smallest patio I'd ever seen, but it had three solid walls, and the house gave it its fourth.

Still, I didn't like the house's place. It stood in a wall of houses that pushed one against the next along a road of dust. A hill rose up behind the patio's back wall, and above was another street and another wall of houses. My family had no plot to grow a single thing to eat.

I knew that Aunt and my cousins all got their due from the marketing, so I wasn't frightened. Yet I wondered: Why live in a bowl, even a great eating bowl like La Paz? Llamas and mules and trucks brought in feasts and feasts. Uncountable thousands came up from the Yungas or down from the high plain of Kollasuyo. Even so, food does not *grow* in a bowl. La Paz had no long bean rows of its own. No one dug for potatoes. I felt far away from Pachamama.

As I settled, Basilia asked, "How did you get here?"

I found a bit of anger. I'd felt it before on that same day, a moment after finding Dionisio. When I turned back to call Simona, I saw her hurrying away. She still feared that Masuru's whispers would find her in La Paz, and she quickly lost herself among people and people.

Why should my family whisper against her? "Juana Páez brought me here. Her daughter Simona helped me find you."

"The twin?" Basilia asked.

"My best friend in the country. A twin who turned bad luck into good!"

Aunt and my cousins looked at me, then among themselves, then back to me. They'd never heard my confronting soul.

I'd never heard it either.

Two days later, Adela and Simona and I—all three of us together—went looking for my town clothes. Adela carried bolivianos, each one holding the power of a hundred centavos. Aunt said there would be enough for a bowler, skirts, and top.

We turned onto La Paz's biggest road, and all of our steps stopped in the same moment. Along the street stood people—hundreds, all pushed one against the next.

A truck among them screamed *biiiii biiiii,* trying to scare a path for itself. It still moved no faster than an old man walks. The soldiers inside surprised me. They weren't angry; they were smiling. Some of the people around them were singing.

We reached this lake of people just as another truck came the other way. I think it had just come down the slopes into La Paz. "Hey!" one of its soldiers shouted. He *was* angry. "What's the commotion?"

"Truce!" someone yelled back.

"When?"

"Noon."

The scowling soldier suddenly showed a soul of glee.

"What does it mean?" I called to him.

He spoke easily. He'd forgotten his anger completely. "It means I won't be shot at again. Maybe I won't be taking supplies to the Chaco at all. If the truce holds, it's the end of the Chaco War."

I prayed. La Paz people prayed, and we kept praying. Maybe all us praying at once touched the Virgin of Copacabana and Jesus and the mountain grandfathers and the saints. No one prayed for Chaco land anymore. Instead of our people praying against the Guaraní, maybe all prayed for the war to end. Maybe one prayer from everyone together was easier to hear.

I never once heard of wide planting fields in the Chaco. So why should there have been war at all over such lands? Basilia told me that Salamanca had wanted new oil fields. Everyone said that oil *might* lie under the Chaco—still, no one was sure. And what was it? Dionisio explained: "It's part of the tribute that trucks want."

I only understood one thing. My confronting soul finally let me see why Salamanca had wanted his name to be a song. It had smiled for him, like the pretending mask of a trickster. He'd wanted it to hide a heart that grew more wicked with every beat.

Three days after the truce, Juana and Simona came to Uncle's house for the feast of Corpus Christi. I wanted them to because the next day they were returning to the country. It was a small feast, but a happy one. Juana and Aunt talked and talked about Father. "I'll look again for him at Masuru," Juana said.

I knew I was lucky to have her and Simona as friends. I still worried that one of my cousins would begin whispering about bad luck, but not one ever did. Maybe they'd stopped fearing Simona. Or maybe they were more afraid of Bartolina Ch'oke's hardest eyes.

July–September 1935

S ometimes Dionisio brought home market papers that Don Emilio was finished with. He spread them on the patio stones and slowly spoke with Spanish words, just as they were woven. "Paraguayan forces have removed to ..."

"What does it mean?"

Dionisio didn't understand everything, but he said that Paraguay was the land of the Guaraní and that the Guaraní and our men had begun to march apart. For a time, we worried only about the distance between the two armies. Later we wondered when the first conscripts, men like Father and Uncle, would be excused to come home.

I found Dionisio on the patio early one morning leaning over a market paper, the same one he'd taken words from the night before. "Does it say more?"

"It always says more, Bartolina. Look at all the words." He turned piece after piece, each a wide white leaf covered with marks and marks of black. Some were as big as the puma faces I'd woven into caps. Most were tiny, more delicate than the smallest flowers on Doña Hilde's skirts.

"What do all the words say?"

"Mostly *wirajjocha* things. This and this person visited some *wirajjocha* house. Here it says more young *wirajjocha*

have found themselves in trouble for criticizing too loudly."
I thought of the ones I'd seen chanting.

"Aaai, here's something! A landslide overran the road I
take to the Yungas."

"How will you go?"

"Tomás knows roads and roads. He'll find a clear one. He
even knows one past Cauquimarca and through passes north
of Macata, but we never go that way. It takes too long."

Dionisio turned another wide leaf. I saw his lips moving
as he took up new words and gave them to himself.

"Dionisio, how do you see the words? I look and look,
but I only see little black stitches."

"It's hard at first. You have to look piece by piece at each
word. Now I can see a whole word in a single instant, but
that wasn't so when the Baptist first showed me. I thought
I'd never—Bartolina, what's wrong?"

"That Baptist is dangerous! You were lucky to get away."

"What are you talking about?"

I told him about Fortunato's warning. A moment later,
my cousin was laughing hard.

"Don't be so brave, Dionisio! Did you ever look closely
at his eyes? They hold blue sky."

"He's strange to look at. You're right about that. He's
even more strange to hear, but he never once acted like a
condor."

"See, he tricked you!"

"Do I look like picked-over bones? That Baptist only
wanted two things. He wanted everyone to call everyone else
Brother, and he especially wanted prayers for Jesus. That's
why he taught words-on-paper. D'you see? Some words-on-
paper belong to Jesus, and the Baptist thought that seeing
them would make me want to say more prayers."

"He didn't speak against Padre Roberto?"

"He *did* speak against Padre Roberto. Think a moment,

Bartolina. That priest wants prayers to the Virgin, prayers to every saint. The Baptist wants prayers *only* for Jesus."

"You stopped prayers to the Virgin and the saints? And to Pachamama?"

Dionisio shrugged. "Didn't Padre Roberto scold when he heard prayers to the grandfather of Illampu?"

"He never scolded me. I only prayed to the saints when he was near."

"There you have it, and it was the same with the Baptist. Outside his mission, I prayed as I pleased. But inside he was teaching me the words-on-paper, so I called him Brother and said prayers for Jesus. I owed him his due, and it's all he ever wanted."

"You're lucky he didn't feel hungry with you sitting there. What then?"

"Bartolina, don't you see why the administrator told Fortunato to spread that condor lie?"

Don Luciano? Why should Dionisio name him when I hadn't? Why should he be so sure of things that he hadn't seen? And yet . . . "Maybe the administrator wanted to scare me away because the Baptist spoke against Padre Roberto."

"Maybe he's afraid of people who learn enough to handle a manifest."

That surprised me.

"Without words-on-paper, how would we have found a living in La Paz? Don Luciano would have loved hearing us ask to return. He would have made Father beg in front of everyone until every single Masuru man stood shaking. What family would give the slightest thought to quitting the hacienda after that?"

Adela and I helped Aunt sell fruit in the market. We learned to tell things—one of us after the other—to make sniffing women want to buy.

"Look at this orange."

"What a size."

"And fresh!"

"Brought quickly from the Yungas by truck."

Working there once, I heard a cry. The woman who'd been selling tin plates across the street left everything sitting and rushed toward four men in the street. They wore the clothes of soldiers but had no rifles or helmets.

The woman only cared about one. I saw her arms seize him. I heard her weeping. I knew without anyone saying it that she was his mother and he was a conscript just excused by the army.

I went running, too. I called out the names of Father and Uncle. All the men listened, but they only shook their heads. Other people heard me and began shouting names. The whole time, the mother held her son—sobbing into his chest, never hearing the calling of names and names all around her.

The market papers began saying that most of the conscripts would be home by the feast of the Nativity. I longed for it to be true. I could only think of Uncle and Father. Two months after the truce, Dionisio took Adela and me to stand in another lake of people. We watched the strangest road anywhere. It seemed to be an iron fence, but lying flat and with no end to it. Mothers scolded if children went too near.

I went stiff when Adela pointed to a giant truck that kept to that road. I heard it taking great breaths and saw it pulling tens and tens of huge carts. Dionisio laughed at my trembling, and I tried to hide my fearing soul. The moment the carts stopped, everyone pushed close around them. The conscripts could hardly step off.

"All those faces!" I said to Dionisio. "How will we find him?"

"Doesn't Father know the way to his own house?" my cousin asked. "If we miss him, we'll find him there."

But I was thinking of *my* father. Dionisio had said that he might come through La Paz, since Masuru was part of its department. But if he passed without seeing us, he might go all the way back to Masuru. Well, he'd find out about me from Concevida, but how would *I* know about *him?*

Everyone said "when he returns," but I worried. He'd been at Nanawa, and who could say he hadn't been dead for two years like Evaristo Páez? If a soldier returned with stones from his grave, would Juana or Concevida send news quickly? If he lived, would he come to La Paz?

I worried that I wouldn't know about Father until Juana returned the next year. That's why I watched so closely. Dionisio looked. Adela looked. We searched and searched those faces, but even so, I knew we weren't seeing them all.

We didn't see Uncle or Father come off those first carts. Later, whenever we heard of men returning, one or two of us went looking. We went every time until the market papers said that no more conscripts were left in the army. We never saw Father, but Uncle Jacinto stepped off a cart a few days before the feast of the Nativity.

September 1935–May 1936

W e Ch'okes all wanted Uncle's stories from the Chaco, so the day after his return he gathered us on the patio. Why start with sandals? But I pointed the moment he sat on a stool and raised a foot across his knee. Deep furrows ran this way and back through his black sole. I'd never seen such a sandal, but suddenly I knew its stuff.

"Uncle, it's from a truck."

"You should see what the Chaco does to boots. Only *wirajjocha* officers ever got new ones. Still, we were lucky. Once a truck passed us just as its tire burst. A whole pack of us went running, each man with a sharp knife to take pieces of that tire."

Aunt and Basilia listened from a bench that had the red scars that old iron gets. Dionisio, sitting with Adela and me on the smooth stones, grew impatient. "Tell about the counteroffensive."

"With all the talk after El Carmen, I thought I'd be facing the Guaraní just outside La Paz. Instead, I rode and rode by truck—among the mountains, then down the other side to Sucre. The slopes were steep and covered with green trees, just like the Yungas. I thought I was low then, but on we went, down and down."

"The Chaco is very low?" Aunt asked.

"Low? It's a pit with no sides. Just going there made our heads sting for days. And the sky!" Uncle pointed upward. "I wondered if I'd ever see blue like this again. From the Chaco, I saw only a sky that seemed to have milk stirred in. Near the ground it lost its last trace of blue. I saw only sickly gray. Distant things grew paler and paler until that grayness seized them and they vanished."

Uncle's next words came in a whisper. "It was the same with souls. I saw many men take on the sickness of that Chaco sky. Their souls grew paler and paler. One soul and the next lost themselves in that grayness—until the men died."

If a man fell there, I wondered, would his souls lose themselves to the grayness? Could an unlucky *angelito* sent there by a foolish sister lose *his* souls to the grayness? I was too afraid to speak my questions.

"Father," said Dionisio, "tell about the counteroffensive. Did you kill many of those Guaraní devils? Did you push the rest right out of the Chaco?"

Uncle caught Dionisio with hard eyes. "What do you know about the Guaraní?" His anger surprised my cousin. "I saw them out on the Chaco and in a prison camp near Itaú. Most of them were boys. Their words were strange, but not their faces, Dionisio. If you gave one La Paz clothes, he could be your brother.

"As for taking back the Chaco . . ." Uncle just shook his head. "Battle after battle *they* had pushed *us* back. They seized almost the whole Chaco. Our counteroffensive took back only the least bit—just enough to let our officers boast that they'd won something," Uncle laughed sadly. "We hurt the Guaraní just enough to make their officers forget about our highlands, but their officers could still say they'd won most of the Chaco. So with the *wirajjocha* officers boasting on both sides, the war could finally end."

Adela was puzzled. "The *wirajjocha* officers?"

Uncle nodded. "The officers of the Guaraní were *wirajjocha*, too. That whole Chaco War was a *wirajjocha* fight."

I saw Uncle's pain when I told him that Guillermo Quispe had last seen Father at Nanawa. Days later, after the army sent home the last conscripts, he took me walking.

"When you came to La Paz, Cristina said that my house was yours, too. Now I'm repeating her words."

I was glad for his kindness, but I thought of an obligation that would be forgotten if I stayed in La Paz. "When I was small, Father and Grandmother and I took feasts to my mother's grave. We did it on All Souls' Day the first three years after she died. Grandmother said that it was especially important then because Mother was still close to the living."

Uncle understood. "And now you worry about your father."

"If he fell at Nanawa, the next All Souls' Day will be his third among the dead. I won't have another chance to be a good daughter while he's still close to the living. Maybe I should go looking for his grave in the Chaco."

I wanted Uncle to scold me for saying that Father might be dead. I wanted him to say that we'd just missed him on his way back to Masuru.

He didn't. "Could you ever find his grave in that wide Chaco? Wait and see what news Juana Páez brings."

Then he faced me, his big hands holding my shoulders. "Bartolina, I think she'll say that a veteran brought stones from his grave. But maybe Donato's souls will follow the stones back. D'you see? We can still visit Cauquimarca someday and honor Donato there."

"But the third All Souls' Day will be past."

"Even so, Bartolina, we have to wait."

I wept, but Uncle was right. All of us wanted to visit our

old cemetery, maybe for Father and surely for Grandfather Alfonso. But Dionisio didn't yet know how to handle a truck. Walking would have kept us out of La Paz for too many days.

I felt a great sadness when that All Souls' Day came. I watched Illimani's three peaks and wondered if I should pray to one grandfather or three. I hadn't seen my Illampu or prayed to its grandfather since sinking into the huge bowl that held La Paz. I felt foolish praying to Pachamama from a place that covered her with stone streets, houses and houses, patios and patios.

I always helped in the market, but my souls seemed mostly to think of Masuru. With each change of the moon, I remembered the bean planting or the pulling of thief shoots, whatever Masuru people needed to do for that season.

Whenever I saw market women showing wide blankets, I remembered Grandmother leaning over her weaving frame. Hadn't she always reminded me that the Ch'okes were the oldest family at Masuru? Sometimes I felt glad to be away from the *mayordomos,* the strange Baptist, and Grandmother's rage, but mostly I felt ashamed that I had fled, leaving no Ch'okes at Masuru.

Sometimes I thought about Doña Hilde. Her words about the grave jumping showed me that she hated Masuru, but I should have known it before. Didn't she rage against dust? Isn't dust the same as Pachamama's soil in its tiniest batches? I wondered if the *patrón* also hated Pachamama. I remembered the time he kept his hands away when Don Luciano showed him the soil. Why, then, should it serve him?

I asked Uncle, but he would only say, "I'm finished with anything to do with that *patrón.*"

Uncle seemed happy to help with the unloading of Don

Emilio's baskets. Tomás was teaching him to handle the truck, and that excited him. More than once he spoke thankfully about the Baptist. Everything had started with the woven words the Baptist had taught Dionisio. I saw their joy, but I wasn't sure the Baptist should be thanked—or trusted. Without the Baptist, maybe Ch'okes would still be at Masuru, maybe enough to call for an uprising.

I surprised myself! Why think about an uprising? Don Luciano seemed so strong.

Still, my confronting soul remembered things. Hadn't the administrator failed to stop the trucks from taking Fortunato Herrán? Hadn't he hushed Doña Hilde rather than risk trouble by stopping the jumping? I also remembered his worry when his son let Guillermo Quispe seize a pistol. And when Rómulo trembled at seeing Grandfather Juan's weapons, Don Luciano's brave words had come only after he saw that the slings and spear shafts were rotten.

I didn't think Salamanca would ever do more harm, but long after his arrest, his whip bit me one last time.

Many months after walking with Uncle, I waited for Juana's return. I wanted good news, but I stood ready to hear about stones from Father's grave.

Juana and Simona came back to La Paz and found us in the market a few days after the feast of the Holy Cross. At first, shadows from their bowlers fell across their faces. But Juana took hers off when they sat with Aunt and me among our baskets of peaches. The moment I found her eyes, I knew that Father had not returned to Masuru.

I could see her pain. I wanted to be kind. Why make her say terrible news? "It's the stones, then?" I asked. That way, she'd only have to nod.

Simona began to weep, and Juana spoke through her own tears. "Bartolina, I asked Concevida as soon as we returned to the country last year. Well, all the conscripts weren't back yet. So I went again just a week ago. I spoke to every Chaco veteran at Masuru." She just shrugged and wiped a tear.

I almost shouted, "What did they say?"

Simona took my hand. "After Guillermo's news, there was never a word more about those first twenty men called to the Chaco. No one can say what happened to them."

June 1936

A month later, Aunt sent me to trade centavos for a red pepper. We expected the men back from the Yungas the next day, and she wanted spice for a chicken plate. On a market street, I stood deciding which pepper was nicest.

A cook looking at corn spoke to the market woman. "They're saying more men are due from Asunción today."

The market woman shook her head. "Always they say more. Always a thousand poor widows go running to meet the smallest truck. That truce was a year ago. What soldier wouldn't be back by now?"

"They say the last prisoners are still coming."

I touched the cook's arm. "Please, Mother, who are these prisoners? Men from the Chaco War?"

"Yes."

"Didn't I say?" said the market woman. "The least word, and everyone's heart goes racing. Girl, I'm very sorry about your father, but—"

I wouldn't hear her. "When are these men coming?" I asked the cook. "Where will they stop?"

"I heard they're coming to La Paz—sometime today."

"What place in La Paz? The rail station?"

"For a truck?"

The market woman grew angry. "Let her shop!"

I forgot the pepper and turned away. I could only think of Father. That same moment, my eyes found a pile of market papers across the street. A woman was selling them at the door of a place where *wirajjocha* went in and out.

I ran and asked her, "Do these say anything about men coming from the Chaco?"

"You have to buy one and see."

"If I put down centavos, will you tell me what it says?"

"Girl, I just sell these. I can't tell what they say."

I felt anger. Why should Dionisio be away just then? I wondered if I could find the secret of the inkweaving myself—right there in the market. Without a weaving soul?

"Do you want one or not?" asked the woman.

Maybe seeing words was different from making them. I could still see a woven llama image. Why not woven words? I hadn't been able to see them before, but maybe I needed to try harder. Dionisio had said it was difficult at first. "What must I put down?"

"Ten centavos."

Aunt would be mad if I came home with no pepper and no centavos, but I had to know. I gave the centavos and took the market paper to a shady place. I pulled it up close to my eyes, but part of it fell away. The lazy brother Wind tried to steal it, and I had to stamp my foot over it quickly! I began again with the rest, looking closely at the big marks. Dionisio had said that at first the only way was to look at each shape carefully. I tried. I looked and looked. I found the shapes but not the words, not a single one. Nothing told me anything about men from the Chaco. I felt sadness and fury, both in the same moment.

Still, I wasn't ready to give up my market paper. I didn't

know how to make it flat again, so I squeezed it under one arm. With the lazy brother teasing, it was like carrying a chicken that might think to fly at any moment.

Instead of going back to Aunt for a scolding about centavos, I followed the widest street in all La Paz, just looking at faces. Some looked back, and if they were *wirajjocha*, I looked away quickly. Some seemed angry, as though they knew about the wasted centavos.

I came to a plaza, the one below the building that wanted to be a mountain. Young *wirajjocha* were there again. This time they weren't shouting. They just walked calmly in and out of the building. Every single one had books! Any of them could take words from a market paper.

I wanted to ask, but my fearing soul warned that they might not want to be fussed. I stood watching for the longest time.

A woman came out one of the doors and sat against the low wall along one side of the plaza. The whole time I watched her, this *wirajjocha* kept a book open in her lap. She never looked up—until my shadow touched it. Her hand went over her face so she could see me without the sun.

"Señorita, please, I need to hear the words this paper holds. I'm trying to find my father."

"Sit down here and tell me what you are talking about."

Her name was María. I told her every single thing, from Salamanca's first trucks right to the moment I put down centavos for the paper. "My aunt told me to trade them for a pepper."

María took hold of the market paper. She knew how to make it obey, the whole thing at once. She looked. She turned pieces of it over. She looked and looked.

"Here."

I almost gasped. "What are the words?"

"This is by telegraph from Sucre: 'Two trucks of the International Red Cross arrived here from Asunción yesterday carrying thirty-four Bolivian soldiers.' "

"Arrived in La Paz? Yesterday?"

"Yesterday, but in Sucre."

"How can I find Sucre?"

"Hush! Listen to the rest: 'The former prisoners of war, one corporal and the rest privates, were honorably discharged from the army upon their arrival in Sucre. The army announced that nineteen of the privates, those from La Paz Department, will be driven by truck to the central depot in La Paz. They are expected to arrive this afternoon.' "

"Does it say their names? Does it say 'Donato Ch'oke'?"

"No, I've told you everything it says."

"Where is the depot?"

"Not far." I listened to every word as she told the way. When she was done, she said, "Here, I will give you back your ten centavos for the paper."

"Thank you, Doña María." Then I was running.

"Bartolina!" she called. "I will say a prayer that you find your father."

My heart raced. But it had raced before, the day I'd called Father's name to that first returning soldier. I wondered if Uncle or Dionisio knew about returning prisoners. Maybe they did. Maybe they hadn't spoken because they didn't want my heart racing again.

The depot was a wide, low building with an iron fence. Finding it wasn't hard because of the people standing outside the fence—all the way around. There were a hundred and a hundred more, mostly women, all waiting to look among those nineteen men.

I went to one woman to ask, but before I could speak, she answered, "Not yet." Hardly anyone said anything else. I wondered how so many people could be so quiet. I waited and watched as others came. They made a stream flowing into that lake of women. That lake of widows?

Maybe I was being foolish. I worried that I wouldn't get back to Uncle's house before dark. I knew that Aunt would be frightened for me, but what could I do?

Then everyone's ears heard a bellowing. Everyone's eyes seized a green truck with a pen covered with cloth. "Let me through," the truck man called as soon as he got close. "Do as I say! Then we can get these men off."

In an instant, we were all around the truck. Those women nearest the truck pulled down the cloth cover. They almost toppled some of the men under it. People shouted out names. "Has Pepe Egaña returned?" "Juan Garro?" "Mariano Nuñez?" The truck man gave up trying to get into the station.

My eyes held one man with the side of his face turned to me. The father who rode away from Masuru four green seasons and three ice seasons before had not been so old as this man. There hadn't been so much gray in his hair, such deep lines in his face. Yet I saw enough to make me scream with all my strength: "Father! Donato Ch'oke!"

He turned the same instant he heard his name.

June–September 1936

My ear pressed against Father's chest as I held him. For a time I heard only his beating heart and my own whispers of thanks to a small saint who had turned bad luck into good.

Even so, Casimiro could only do so much. He had protected Father every single moment. Why should anyone expect more of him in a place like Nanawa? And so all around us the calling of names kept on—excited shouts at first, finally sorrowful cries.

Father stayed at the depot and listened to every woman who came asking a name. Some asked two names. One asked *five*. Father sadly answered that one man had died of a snake bite. That was the only news he could give anyone.

A week later a truck brought another seven men. No more ever returned from the Chaco War.

Father told of long marches in search of water. "When the slightest rain fell, we knelt around puddles—sometimes just patches of mud. We dampened rags torn from our sleeves and squeezed out a few drops to wet our mouths. Sometimes the least bit of damp mud made us think it was a feast day."

We heard about El Carmen, where the Guaraní had

seized Father. He spoke of the prison camp in Asunción. "A green season passed, then an ice season, and then another green season. We who weren't moaning with illness learned cards and checkers and played with the Guaraní. Even after the truce, we waited and waited while *wirajjocha* shouted one against the other over peace."

When Dionisio asked about Nanawa, Father told him almost nothing. I thought, Maybe he worries that Nanawa talk will make Juana Páez weep.

Simona's mother came each day to hear Father. She trembled to his words about guns so big that they needed trucks to pull them. She put her hand on his when he moaned about not planting a single bean row season after season.

We wondered why Juana waited in La Paz beyond her time for going back to the country. Once, she stayed and listened while Father talked of a *wirajjocha* named Diego, the same man that Guillermo Quispe had told me about. In that La Paz plaza, long before I ever saw it, Diego had chanted against Salamanca's war.

"He shouted once too often," Father said. "Soon he found himself in the Chaco, marching in an Aymara troop."

Juana gasped. "The *wirajjocha* always said that it was an honor to march for Bolivia! Since when is a disrespectful son punished with an honor?"

She was raging. That *was* something to be mad about, but no one had ever seen quiet Juana even the least bit angry. Soon we were all laughing. Even Father's smile returned for the first time since the war.

A few days later, he carried a load of firewood to Juana's people in La Paz. Simona and I followed—just far enough back to keep him from seeing.

"That wood came all the way from the Yungas," I said.

"Did he put down some of his war pay for it?"

"I think we're going to be like sisters, Simona."

* * *

Why should Pachamama serve a faraway *patrón* who stands back from her soil? Sitting as a prisoner in Asunción, the *wirajjocha* Diego had wondered this same thing that I wondered. I know, because noisy Diego always wondered with his tongue, and Father had listened and listened.

On our last day in La Paz, Father made a vow. He said that before he died even the *patrón* would admit that part of Masuru belonged to Ch'okes.

Uncle wanted Father to settle in La Paz. "Here's where people spoke against the war, even *wirajjocha* students. Here's where we hear talk about justice, about land rights. Donato, go back to Masuru, and you'll never hear such talk again."

"If I don't stand with Pachamama, how can I ever claim the land?"

They spoke and spoke. When Uncle still saw Father's certain eyes, he said only one more thing. "After Julia's revolt, maybe you'll find trouble with Don Luciano when you go back. Or maybe someday you'll find your suffering is too great. Then I hope you'll remember that the Ch'okes in La Paz will always welcome you."

Dionisio gave us an old manifest with a new inkweaving he'd made on its clean side. "If you ever need to send word to us, take this to the Baptist in Cauquimarca."

I took it, but my fearing soul whispered a warning.

My cousin—a town man now, who thought no one was wiser—watched my eyes. "Trust the Baptist, Bartolina. He'll help."

Father wanted to reach Masuru before the first planting. We climbed out of the great bowl, Juana and Simona with us, eight days before the feast of the Nativity. The sun sank while we walked between Chipamaya and Batallas, so we wrapped ourselves in blankets and slept a little way off the road.

I awoke in the night. A thin moon had followed quickly after the sun, so even the smallest stars came looking. I could hear Juana whispering.

"Did he suffer?" Father was silent, and Juana asked again. "What happened to Evaristo?"

"As Guillermo said, he fell . . . at Nanawa."

"Say whatever you can about it."

In the slightest whisper Father told of the Guaraní sheltered in their fort. Salamanca's guns-behind-trucks shook the Chaco with their shots, but still the Guaraní wouldn't flee. "During a lull, the captain sent Evaristo and Guillermo sneaking forward. He wanted to know about patrols, but I think a patrol found them first. Guillermo crawled back, bleeding and almost dead, moaning that Evaristo had fallen. He was carried to the rear, and I never saw him again."

"If Guillermo was wounded so badly just as Evaristo fell, how could he bring me stones from Evaristo's grave?" For the longest time I heard only breathing, then: "Donato, I've heard talk of Nanawa in the markets. I know that Guillermo spoke kindness, not truth. What happened?"

"Those biggest guns went silent. We had no more shells for them. Men with rifles had to go forward, even with the Guaraní firing down from the fort. Siege after siege, Juana—men and men falling with each one! We couldn't breach that fort. Yet the officers kept ordering and ordering until only a few of us remained to hear.

"We finally dropped back. We worried that the Guaraní would attack us, so I sneaked back to watch them. A few left the fort. I saw three standing with a gasoline can at the bottom of a . . . hill."

I had never heard what I did then—Father weeping. Finally he whispered again. "It was a hill of the dead. The Guaraní had gathered men and men and men. Even so, hundreds of others lay all around just where they'd fallen. I don't have numbers for them all. I just remember those three Guaraní trying to burn that first hill of the dead. . . ."

"Donato?"

"They couldn't keep the fire alive! I prayed to the saints to let it burn, but it was no good. Those Guaraní finally went running, hands over their mouths."

Juana and Father sobbed, maybe until they slept. I lay hating Salamanca for stealing our men and sending them to fall in a land barren even of graves.

I thought of two other *wirajjocha*, María and Diego, but I was afraid. Maybe too few were like them.

Lying there near the road, my fearing soul seized me with other worries, all the ones I'd forgotten during my year in La Paz. What about the whips? What about Grandmother's rage against me? And what if Father, whom I'd just heard weeping, was too weak to make the *patrón* hear his vow?

And what about that strangest of all men? Should the Baptist be counted among the kind *wirajjocha* or the wicked *wirajjocha*? Should he be counted among the *wirajjocha* at all? Dionisio trusted him, but my fearing soul did not.

Yet hadn't the secret of the inkweaving made Dionisio strong? I lay wondering about its power. I began thinking about what I might do at Masuru—about what I *had* to do.

We stopped near Huarina to see Tulio. Juana's uncle looked surprised when we said we were going back to Masuru.

"Don Luciano knows the hacienda families well," he told Father. "He knows you're brother to Jacinto Ch'oke, who made trouble. He knows Bartolina is grandchild to Cara-navis. Maybe he won't let you back."

Juana worried, too. "Even when I went looking for you the last time, families and families were asking about land.

The war sent everyone moving about. Who can say how many might be asking to settle at Masuru? We should rush back."

"I want to find things out first," Father said. The next day he went alone to Cauquimarca.

"We'll go to Masuru tomorrow?" Juana asked when he returned.

Father shook his head. "Why go rushing? We'll wait a few days and arrive during the feast of the Nativity."

Early on that feast day, I wrapped myself in the old shawl with the llama train. Before the sun was high, we were kneeling among the Ch'oke graves. I begged Grandfather Alfonso to forgive me for not coming on his first All Souls' Day among the dead. I appeased him with coca and happy news about our family living safely in La Paz.

We took the road into Masuru and found the families gathered in the near pasture. The sound of drums and pipes rushed through my ears. All that music made me think of the feasts from days before we'd ever heard of the Chaco. The men and older boys danced, and the women and girls chanted the wordless songs. I wondered who could provide so much food and *chicha*.

I saw Doña Hilde under a wide hat. A white cloth over it was tied beneath her frown. Even on feast days, she hated Masuru. Don Luciano was with her, and so was an old *wirajjocha* man I didn't recognize.

This old man had trousers and a shirt of smooth and very white cloth. A Masuru girl held an umbrella to shade him. Like Doña Hilde, he didn't want the sun to see his face. He wasn't tall, and from the shape of him I could see he had never been hungry—not for a single day in his life. I thought he must be the feast sponsor, maybe a wealthy guest of the administrator.

Don Luciano and Doña Hilde nodded each time he said anything, and when wasn't he saying something? He stopped only to greet any hacienda family that came smiling.

Father went forward and said something to the sponsor, maybe greeting him. Just then the musicians began a rest, and I could hear everything else being said. Everyone could, for Father spoke Aymara words in a strong voice. "For three years I have served in the army. Now I return to take up the same land that my father and his father worked."

"Donato!" It was a shout of joy from Concevida. "By the Virgin's hand, look. Donato Ch'oke has come through the war alive." With so many people about, some didn't know until then that Father had returned.

One was Don Luciano. I saw his anger, but it quickly hid, and he greeted Father with Aymara words. "What a blessing that you've come away from the war safely." He turned to the sponsor and spoke Spanish words. "Donato lost his wife—years ago. He doesn't have any family left here. I don't know if it is wise for a man alone to take a plot, *Patrón.*"

Patrón! The breath stopped in my lungs.

Father took in those words. Then he surprised Don Luciano—and me. I didn't know until that moment that he'd learned to hear Spanish words. But he still spoke with Aymara words for everyone else. "You'll be happy to learn, Don Luciano, that Juana Páez, whose husband fell in the Chaco in service to Bolivia, has returned with me. We each bring a daughter. We can offer what any family can."

He raised his voice even more. "I have war bolivianos that will bring eight sheep from the Achacachi market. I'll give one for the feast of La Merced—if I settle here."

"Why wouldn't you, Donato?" called Concevida. Others began shouting the same thing. I began to see Father's strength.

Don Luciano spoke more Spanish words to the *patrón.* "Donato is the son-in-law to Julia Caranavi."

The *patrón* went stiff, just for the smallest moment. He spoke for the first time. "That worries me, Donato. Don't think I don't know that old Julia tried to start an uprising last year."

"I'm sorry for that trouble, *Patrón,* but on that day I was in a prison camp near Asunción. I was there because I went to fight Bolivia's war."

I'd never heard such a silence at a festival. The musicians forgot their music. Like everyone, they stood listening to every last word.

Don Luciano spoke loudly with Aymara words. "The *patrón* won't tolerate trouble. There is no place—"

The *patrón's* hand, just its slightest movement, silenced the administrator.

"Don Luciano speaks correctly," he said. "Donato, Masuru people want to go about their business peacefully. As a favor to them, I won't stand for the least bit of trouble."

"*Patrón,* I fought at Nanawa *and* El Carmen." Concevida heard this and called to the saints. Father finished: "After such sorrow, why would I go looking for more?"

The *patrón* put a hand to his chin. "So, Donato, you want to come back to the land? You and your family know how to work hard?"

Six men all shouted answers to him: "Donato Ch'oke? Has Masuru ever seen a harder worker?"

The *patrón* turned to Don Luciano, who only shrugged. Still, I saw the administrator's eyes. He was holding back a soul of anger.

The *patrón* rubbed his chin. Everyone waited for his next words, and finally he called to a *mayordomo.* "See to it that these Ch'okes get settled."

Then he looked all around. "I've come all this way to sponsor a feast. What's happened to the music?" The next hours were given to drums and pipes.

September 1936

While the musicians still played, I found the curer
Arturo and told him what I wanted.

"Ha!" he scolded. "Don't you see I'm having my *chicha*?"
Arturo had a frightful look. He wore a tiny hat. Even its
brim was too small to shade his face, and his old, dry skin
stretched tightly over sharp cheekbones. I thought they'd
break through if he ever smiled.

"Please, Grandfather, if you help me, I'll weave you a cap
with a puma face on each earflap." I remembered that
curers liked things in threes. "I'll put a third one on the
front."

He looked at the llama train on my shawl. "Did you weave
this?"

"Yes, Grandfather."

"Then go to the cemetery. I'll follow soon."

Up the road, just outside the stone wall, I knelt among
the graves of thieves. Beside the grave of Grandfather Juan
lay a new grave, as I knew one would.

"Grandfather and Grandmother," I said, "your people
are back at Masuru." I told every last thing that had happened to Father. I remembered the hill of the dead and
spoke of the *wirajjocha* Diego. Next I told of my own time
in La Paz. I explained that the *wirajjocha* María had helped

~ 129 ~

me find Father. I didn't leave a single thing out. I even said that Simona and I were like sisters.

"These are days when twins can turn bad luck into good. These are days when young *wirajjocha* will sometimes point the way. And did you hear Father when he faced the *patrón* today? These are days when an obliging soul and a confronting soul can stand strong together.

"It's true! Father used obliging words to ask for the land, but did you listen? Don Luciano didn't want us back. Father confronted him with the *patrón* standing right there, with all the Masuru people standing right there. Father had his way, and he says that before he dies, even the *patrón* will agree that some Masuru land belongs to the Ch'okes."

The curer came walking just outside the wall. I spoke more things quickly to my grandparents: "We haven't forgotten our land rights. No one has—just look."

All around both of their graves lay woven flowers and bits of coca leaf. "Masuru people still honor you."

Arturo circled me with a slow dance. He'd changed his cap and now wore a magic one with earflaps hanging well past his shoulders. I could hear him mumbling.

I leaned close to Grandmother's grave. "I need to weave. I won't tell lies; I might need it to make things for the *patrón*. But I need it for more than that. There's a new weaving, a weaving that made my cousin Dionisio strong. That same weaving can let me stand with Father and help him keep his vow. Let me have my weaving soul. Oh, please."

"Julia!" This was Arturo calling. "I bring coca for you and Juan." Between the graves he stacked three full leaves, dull sides down, shining green sides up. He ground them into shreds with a stone. "I bring you *chicha*." He spilled a bit for my grandparents from a tiny flask. "But I only hear Bartolina's softest little voice. 'Oh, pleeeease,' she says."

This mocking angered my confronting soul. That same soul—the one Grandmother most respected—made my voice sound like a *mayordomo*'s whip. "Grandmother, free my weaving soul!"

That same moment Arturo stepped close. He looked everywhere—to the sky, to the soil, to the mountains. "Bartolina!" he called.

I was surprised. Couldn't he see me? I was kneeling right there and began to tell him so. Swiftly, his hand covered my mouth. Arturo went on shouting and shouting my name. Then he pulled away my shawl and beat it against the ground. "Bartolina! Bartolina Ch'oke!"

The curer stretched out a long finger over Grandmother's grave. He touched a spot where the *chicha* had dampened the soil. The smallest sandy grains clung to the finger, and he held them to my face. "Eat."

I pulled my head back, but his finger followed. "Eat!" Then I felt the roughness on my tongue, the cracking of tiny grains between my teeth. I closed my eyes and swallowed.

Not an hour after Arturo called back my weaving soul, I stood along the road just past Cauquimarca's square. The Baptist's black truck stood there, too, just as it had the time once before when I'd come looking. Again its two glass eyes seemed to hold me.

But I had ridden in trucks since then. I knew none ever sprang without someone inside to provoke it. I moved close enough to see dust clinging to the huge round eyes, making them dull. Not even the dust feared a truck standing quiet.

I went to the Baptist's door, but just then I heard a clod crusher breaking up the soil. I followed close along the side of the house and peered past its corner. I silently watched the Baptist, who stood facing away.

~ 131 ~

If the Baptist *is* counted among the *wirajjocha*, he is the only one I ever saw pleasing Pachamama with such care and kindness. I watched him breaking the clods and digging the furrows on his little plot. He did every single thing that Pachamama wanted. So why not give her prayers?

I didn't try to understand. I just searched for the same trust that Dionisio held for the Baptist.

I had wanted to confront Fortunato Herrán. I wanted to ask if his telling about the wicked condor was a lie, then watch his eyes when he answered. But only that day I'd learned that thirst and fever had seized Fortunato. All his souls had lost themselves in the grayness of the Chaco.

I tried to calm my fearing soul, but even my own heart seemed to call out: "Go back. Go back." I should wait, I thought. I should come again when Father can stand with me, maybe in the next ice season, when there are more hours to learn the inkweaving.

The Baptist straightened. I only then realized how old he must be. He moved no more quickly than Grandfather Alfonso had. I saw nothing of the condor in his movement.

"Casimiro," I called, just in the faintest whisper. "I love you for the protection you gave Father. Even before I loved you as my only brother in the world. But have you seen this Baptist? Do you know his customs? Casimiro, I have to follow one—it's no disrespect to you. I just need the inkweaving so that I can help Father keep his vow."

I stepped away from the house to a spot where nothing could hide me, and I called out to the Baptist.

"Brother!"

March 1938

The long table before me has no carvings and does not shine. I look down at the inkweaving Dionisio put into my hands a year and a half ago. I carefully weave its same words onto a pouch of paper the Baptist has given me:

> Señor Dionisio Ch'oke
> By kind favor of Señor Emilio Catari
> Central Postal Station, La Paz

I laugh each time I think about my town cousin calling himself *señor*. But marketing waits for me, so I take a flat leaf with square corners and quickly weave new words:

> My cousin,
>   All the Masuru Ch'okes greet all the La Paz
> Ch'okes. Dionisio, we smile whenever we
> remember the day that you took that long road
> back from the Yungas and stopped in
> Cauquimarca. Grandfather was surely pleased that
> you brought him a feast on his third All Souls'
> Day among the dead. When the harvest is in and
> the ice season begins, I'll go marketing in La Paz
> with Juana. I'll see you again before the feast of
> Corpus Christi.

Why do you worry about the *mayordomos* confronting me over visits to the Baptist? I go in and out on market day, and everyone sees. But the administrator pretends not to. He doesn't want to confront Father because no other Masuru man is more respected. Why risk another defeat over the doings of one quiet girl not yet sixteen?

Manuela says that the administrator intends to leave Masuru one day soon. He doesn't say so, but Doña Hilde moans and moans about being away from Oruro. Because of her, Don Luciano is growing distant from this land—just like the *patrón.*

Father was glad for the La Paz news you brought. He asks for more and more. What is said about land laws? Are the young *wirajjocha* still confronting the old? You can safely send news by kind favor of the Baptist.

Father especially thanks you for telling him about the Achacachi gathering. He went. He saw men from towns and other haciendas. Some he already knew from Asunción, so trust was quick. They all heard a *wirajjocha* man speak about land rights. The man was Father's friend Diego. Casimiro must have led him there!

Father brought home an inkweaving, and he secretly called other Chaco veterans to our house. He had me speak its words for all of them, and these told of a new Achacachi meeting still to come. An Aymara man there will tell how he made a rural union among hacienda farmers near Chipamaya. Father is sending one of our veterans to listen.

I stop and think about our *patrón*. Father says I mustn't repeat the Achacachi news in Masuru. For that, Don Luciano *would* make trouble because an administrator and especially a *patrón* hate talk about rural unions.

My fearing soul worries. Maybe a *mayordomo* will pull away my pouch and show these woven words to Don Luciano.

What then?

I think of Grandmother. I think of my La Paz family, waiting to welcome me if I ever need them. I steady my hand and weave the next stitch.

Afterword

Bartolina Ch'oke, the events she witnesses, and the people she meets are fictional. Cauquimarca and Masuru appear only in this story, but a detailed map of South America will show Achacachi and the mountain peak Illampu. They stand just east of Lake Titicaca and northwest of the great market town La Paz. The Aymara Indians of the region are just as real.

More than a million Aymara are alive today, most of them in Bolivia. Eight hundred years ago, their ancestors built a series of kingdoms on the high Andean plain around the lake. Living on poor soil thirteen thousand feet above sea level, they worked hard to survive against wind, violent hail, and frost, which could come in any month of the year.

Around 1460, the expanding Inca Empire ended Aymara independence. In the 1530s, Spaniards defeated the Incas, and in 1825, Hispanic Bolivians won their independence from Spain. For nearly five hundred years, the Aymara and other Indian groups labored to support this parade of ruling peoples—even as they struggled to survive themselves.

Yet the Aymara preserved their own language and beliefs, such as the existence of four or five souls within each person. The Spaniards imposed Catholicism, and the Aymara appeared to accept it. However, rather than becoming traditional Christians, they merely added Catholic figures to their own large family of deities. Canadian Baptists and other missionaries made significant contributions to education and health, but they rarely won serious converts.

In 1932, Bolivian President Daniel Salamanca provoked the Chaco War, a tragic dispute over lowland plains claimed by both Bolivia and Paraguay. Both sides suffered disastrous casualties, mostly among Indian conscripts, who felt little national identity and who had no stake in the Chaco.

In Bolivia the war became a symbol of the suffering and servitude that the Aymara and other Indian groups had endured for centuries. The outrage that followed doomed the age of the *patrón*.

Many tenant laborers of Donato's generation lived to see land reforms that gave them their own small farms. With the support of Bolivians of all ethnic backgrounds, they and their sons and daughters won civil rights and meaningful citizenship in the 1950s.

About the Author

DAVID NELSON BLAIR has family throughout South America, and as a child, he lived in Bolivia for two years. Armed with this background and a master's degree in Latin American history, he wrote *The Land and People of Bolivia*. His first novel, *Fear the Condor*, was inspired by what he learned about the Aymara people of that country.

Mr. Blair has been a newspaper editor and is now a free-lance copy editor who works with university presses. He lives in Easton, Pennsylvania.